MAELSTROM

MAELSTROM

Southwest Faerie Chronicles

MAGGIE CRITCHLEY

MARQUEZ PRICE, 20 SIDED STUDIOS

M CRITCHLEY

For my father, who gave me Bansalee and, everything else.

Beginning

She watched him sleep while she finished dressing. They had married young and still looked it, as they always would. They are Fae and Faeries are gifted with long life. Some, like Teagan, had other gifts as well. She considered the most precious of hers to be her handsome husband, Rylan, who was fast asleep on the right side of their bed, his side.

March had just settled in and was not yet ready to leave its winter chill behind, so she was dressing warmly. Thick black leggings under thick black socks, she felt the weight of her enchanted bullet proof vest as she put it on over her black thermal under shirt. Pulling her blue sweater dress over her head and zipping up her knee-high black leather boots, she stepped into their bathroom. Turning on the light only after the door was securely shut. She began her pre-work ablutions, brushing her teeth, pulling her unruly scarlet curls into a neat chignon and dusting a bit of powder across her pale skin. It was the middle of the night, and she was only going to work so decided she wouldn't bother with eye makeup for her almond shaped sage green eyes. She flipped off the light before exiting the bathroom and mentally prepared herself for the journey of exploring others' thoughts.

She arrived at the pub a mere 30 minutes after receiving the call out. One of the many perks of what the rest of her world considered her most precious gift, anything related to

the mind she could interpret and command as she saw fit thus, she did not require a briefing before her response to a call as she'd already 'heard' all about it. There was an air of fear about the place, noticeable to her from at least a mile out. Everyone had already been questioned by human detectives and, had been allowed to leave but Teagan was there to get the real story.

The outside of the pub was unremarkable. Red brick walls, blackened wood door (presently broken and hanging from the hinges), aging wooden "Collins' Public House" sign swinging gently in the wind from the rusted chain bolted into the brick.

She continued inside where it was much cozier than the view from the street would lead one to believe. It was rich cherry wood, soft cream-colored cushions on high backed chairs, the smell of leather mixed with pipe tobacco and the largest bar she had ever seen graced the middle of the room with access from all sides of its octagonal shape. Pool and card tables, as well as dart boards, were set up at various points throughout so patrons could entertain themselves if the mood struck. It looked like a rather nice place to enjoy a drink and good company. Pushing through the seemingly pleasant veneer, she began slowly to "read" the room. Closing her eyes, she saw it as it was three hours before she had stepped into it.

"Oi! We need another round over here," shouted a rotund red-faced man above the din. The bartender, dressed in white button-down shirt and black slacks, was working like a demon to keep up with the need for booze being called to him from every angle of the bar. He merely nodded to the gentleman in answer.

A petite woman with long hair of the palest blonde, was sitting on one of the lavish stools at the bar. Standing next to her was a strikingly handsome, very young man with hair black as pitch and eyes the most intense shade of brown. They were engaged in some inane conversation about the crowd. He was desperate for her attention; she was clearly uninterested. He was clearly human; she was definitely a Soul Reaver though not someone Teagan recognized. Augustana Van Dotch? She was perplexed by the fact that she couldn't read the man. He was like a piece of lined paper. Nothing there but exactly what one was looking at.

Suddenly there was a loud crack in the direction of the entrance. It was the door being kicked in and broken off its hinges by a broad man wearing heavy black boots. The next thing Teagan saw after his boot was a bolt shooting from a crossbow pointed at the dark-haired man who was trying to get lucky.

His aim was true and struck the man through the back of his head. The blonde Reaver disappeared in a blur of dove grey satin just as the bolt struck and shortly after another woman screamed and began furiously to search for her cell phone as the dark-haired man fell bleeding against the bar. The assassin turned on his boot and left as quickly as his arrow struck and all Teagan saw was the tail of his brown coat blowing in the wind.

From his thoughts she gathered that he was Andreaus

Dominus, a well-known mercenary often employed by The UnSeelie King. He did not know why he was sent to kill the man, only that he needed killing and the King paid him handsomely to do it.

The bar tender shook his head exasperated at the mess he would undoubtedly have to clean. The other patrons were momentarily dumb struck before realization and subsequent panic set in.

Quickly gathering their things and settling tabs in an attempt to leave before the police could respond. Too late. The Human police presence was announced by their blaring sirens and flashing emergency lights. They never could help themselves making an entrance. They entered with guns drawn and shouting for everyone to stay where they were. Satisfied that all parties present had complied, they set about separating and questioning the thirty-five witnesses, unaware that there should've been thirty-six.

Opening her eyes, she exited the pub and headed to the station to write her report and brief her superiors. She was glad it was some distance away as she wanted to mull over what she had seen and was grateful for fresh air. Toiling through other's thoughts and energy was trying even after a lifetime of doing it. She had figured out how to control her ability in her youth. The ebb and flow of information was constant and blocking others from her mind was the first thing she learned.

To this day her father and husband were the only ones who had accomplished breaching her guard effortlessly. Her father respected her privacy. Rylan was, and always has been, an entirely different story. She was not a particularly private person but tried to keep her thoughts to herself when possible; he came and went as he pleased. She laughed inwardly at the dream he was currently having. Pirates, really? Even 130-year-old Fae are still sprites at their root.

Preventing herself from entering other's thoughts unless bidden, came second. As a young Faerie she often strayed into the minds of those close-by without realizing what she had done. She learned the hard way that she could read every experience a person had once she was inside their head; it was a very frightening and intriguing moment. An adult human, running past her on the playground after his son, had been remembering very vividly a fight he had overheard his parents having when he was small and the resulting abuse, when his father realized what he had overheard. She was paralyzed by his fear. She could taste the blood in her mouth when he was struck, and could smell the strong stench of urine when his fear overwhelmed his four-year-old faculties. He was thinking simultaneously about how grateful he was that he did not continue the cycle of abuse.

It could also be quite embarrassing. She was glad she figured out how to "switch" off her mind before her or her brothers had reached adolescence. She shuddered to think what she may have accidentally been privy to.

Controlling environments came last and was used least often. "It's all about focus," the words of her mentor echoed from long ago, as Teagan smiled at the memory, "tapping into the beings mind and utilizing bits of their own experiences to bind with whatever situation you're building to make it as realistic as possible."

She was transported momentarily from the midwinter

snow in the woods behind her childhood home, to digging her toes into wet sand on a deliciously warm beach she had visited with her family. She could feel the sun on her skin, smell the salt from the sea and hear the whine of seagulls flying overhead. In a heartbeat she was back in the woods about to start her first lesson, not realizing until later that little trick was her first glimpse.

Trinity was an acquaintance of her grandfathers and had a skill similar to her own.

She was an elf, tall and willowy with violet eyes and raven black hair that flowed in gentle waves to the small of her back, though she almost always kept it braided. She was a fierce fighter as well as being able to control minds, and she insisted Teagan know how to fight as well.

"We cannot always rely solely on our gift," she told her before their first fencing lesson, "sometimes a good thrashing is all that will get the message across properly."

She then proceeded to give Teagan a brutal thrashing indeed, the first of many until she became proficient with her katana.

The actual murder wasn't necessarily of note, that had become a frequent enough occurrence. What she was concerned about was the Reaver and the fact that she could not read the murdered human. She had never encountered someone she could not read, especially a human. They were the easiest of beings to read. One could pretty much look at a human and tell what they were thinking.

Teagan could read humans in her sleep. Except this one, unsettling indeed. Perhaps the murder was the message, a "good thrashing" that would certainly speak volumes. What message though and to whom...*From* whom? Why would a Fae King care about the life or, death rather, of a human? Aside from sport, most Fae didn't care for humans in the least. The lady Reaver was the key here, Teagan was sure of it. Augustana Von Dotch would need to be found and questioned. She did not belong to a clan but was familiar to a Knight, Orion, in the Unseelie Court. Finding him would be easy, getting him to give up his lover would be quite another matter. She was unlocking her office door before she knew it and settled in to start her paperwork.

Finishing up her notes, she shut down her computer, stretched her way out of her chair and turned off the lights in her office. Making sure to lock the door as she left, she looked at her watch and realized she would only just make it home in time for breakfast with Rylan before he headed off to work. Such is the life of a Public Servant. Fae or otherwise, odd hours and unpredictable schedules required very patient friends and family.

Teagan was lucky the people in her life seemingly had the patience of saints and happened to love her immensely. Nodding good morning to the few bleary-eyed officers coming on shift, the smell of morning coffee clinging to their uniforms, she quickly exited the building and took to the sky. She wanted to get home as quickly as possible, and her wings were just that.

Feeling the familiar thrum of energy as gravity struggled to do its job, she reveled in the fresh air that rushed past her as she shot upward and began making her way southward home. She loved flying, always had. The first time she used her wings she flipped herself upside down because she lacked control. Now, she did it just because she wanted to. She never felt freer than when she was in the air. No computer, no cell phone, nothing to focus on but the task at hand. It was the only time she wasn't mired in her own or other's thoughts. It was glorious. She loved the sun on her face and when the air smelled of rain, as it did now. Tomorrow most likely and welcome it would be. She avoided birds as she passed them and kept low enough to avoid disturbing any aircraft that may be nearby. Even glamoured as she was, she could be picked up on radar. Human technology had advanced by leaps and bounds since she was small. Not nearly to the point of Fae technology but, not everyone was the genius developer Seth Patrick.

Before long, the home she built and shared with her husband came into view. The whitewashed brick and Solar paneled roof were some of her favorite and more unique attributes they had decided on. Most Fae made their homes in the trees or, at least of wood.

Teagan loved the bricks they had made with their own hands from earth they owned themselves. There was a well-worn stone pathway leading up to the front door which was large enough for two Sumo wrestlers to fit through and made of the strongest cherry wood. It had ancient druidic runes etched in silver down the middle from the top to the bottom and a heavy silver handle her brother had made himself.

There was no keyhole. Seth had used the most advanced fingerprint recognition system as security so, all one needed to do was place their hand on the handle. If you were recognized as a guest of the house, it would open. Otherwise, you would end up with at least one very irate Faerie at your back with a blade to your throat and a lot of explaining to do.

Landing gracefully at their front door, Teagan checked to make sure her phone was on silent mode and placed her hand on the handle. Entering her home, she drank in the familiar sights and smells as she closed the door behind her. The brownies she baked yesterday still permeated the kitchen with the scent of chocolate and caramel. Rylan's cherry pipe tobacco was a constant under current as was the comforting smell of their decades old brown leather couch.

She placed her phone in its charger on the entryway table, unzipped and slid off her boots so she could walk down the hallway as quietly as possible. She could feel that Rylan was still half asleep and did not wish to wake him yet. Peeling off her sweater dress as she went, she held it in one hand and started taking off her vest just as she entered their bedroom and Rylan awoke. Closing the bedroom door, she dropped her dress and vest on the floor as he rolled over to look at her through sleep gummed cornflower blue eyes. She crawled into bed next to him and he gathered her to him.

"Good morning wife," his deep morning rasp greeted her.

"Good morning husband," she replied smiling at him affectionately.

"You know, most husbands would worry that their gorgeous wives stroll in at half past six, half dressed. It's a good thing I know better," he beamed back at her touching his temple and winking at her.

"About that, did you know you still dream about pirates?"

"Did you know all your murder investigating kept interrupting my dreams about pirates?"

"Did it? Sorry darling, some of us have gruesome jobs that keep us from dreaming about pirates all night."

"Sounds like a personal problem. Keep it down next time so I can get to the part about ravishing the beautiful stow away."

"Oh well, I certainly wouldn't want to interrupt that."

"How dare you madam! And here I thought I married a pure and virtuous woman!"

"Did you now? I'd love to meet her."

Placing his hands on either side of her face he kissed her deeply. Freeing her hair from its bun with one hand he steadied himself with the other as she tucked herself beneath him.

"I have to get ready for work," he pouted and kissed her forehead.

"I know," she said pulling her arms out of her shirt sleeves, "we better make it quick then, hadn't we?"

"I like where your heads at McCarthy," he grinned widely.

"I can't say the same of you just yet McCarthy," she said pulling off her shirt the rest of the way and starting on her leggings.

"Give me about 30 seconds and you'll be whistling a different tune," he said against her mouth before he kissed her again and set about his husbandly duties.

Forty-five minutes later, the aroma of frying bacon greeted Rylan as he came strolling into the kitchen fresh from the shower and looking every inch the schoolteacher. He smelled like almond body wash and his familiar vetiver musk, his blond hair gelled perfectly into place. White button-down shirt open to the second button, rolled up to the elbows, tucked into his grey tweed trousers and black suspenders, black converse and an ornery smile completed his ensemble. He took plates from the cabinet and went about setting the table. Grabbing their coffee cups last and taking a long pull from his own, he pulled out her chair as she made her way to the table with their breakfast.

"This is delicious love, thank you", he said around a mouthful of bacon.

She took an appreciative drink of her decaf brew, giving a contented sigh as she exhaled.

"You're welcome, love", she said before digging into her own plate of eggs, bacon and potato pancakes.

They finished their meals in relative silence. Him going through his list of to do's for the week in his head, she interrupting his thoughts to remind him of their family dinner that night and doctor appointment at the end of the week.

"Aye, I remember woman. Now stop pestering me so I can go to work," he teased her as he rinsed his plate and left it in the sink for her. He knew how much she hated him cleaning. No one knew how to do chores properly but Teagan McCarthy.

Nary a house was clean before, nor would be after she was about the world.

"Be gone with you then old man so I can get some sleep", she teased him back.

Hugging each other goodbye and exchanging chaste kisses, he left for work and her to finish cleaning the kitchen.

Monday, Rylan's least favorite day of the week. He had all six of his classes today and none of them would be paying the least bit of attention to him. Today, he was grateful for that, as he felt just as distracted as the adolescents he taught. Bansail Preparatory was within walking distance of the McCarthy's home. It was a charter school for gifted children founded by

Inez Kinsella Patrick in 1712 for her son, Rylan's father-in-law, who showed an unusual aptitude for music at a very young age. Rylan taught English Literature and helped the Theatre department when they needed sets built.

It would be a good few months until their next musical was on, and Rylan was itching to put his skills to good use. Carpentry was one of his favorite hobbies, and it had been a long time since he had built anything of significance. He planned to start on their child's bedroom furniture just as soon as his and Teagan's families knew they were expecting.

He arrived at his classroom just in time for the first bell to sound and was not surprised to see but a few half-asleep human children at their desks, hung over no doubt. Human kids started experimenting much sooner than Fae children or, so it seemed to Rylan. They were also much less responsible and trustworthy though, perhaps only because human adults preferred to remain ignorant of their children's lives and human children had all their fun in secret.

Fae parents encouraged their sprites to experiment in the comfort of their own homes. That way they knew exactly what their offspring were getting into and that they were safe.

There were very few rebellious Fae and even fewer family secrets. In fact, if it weren't for their fantastical nature, mischief would be very hard to come by at all. He set his green leather messenger bag on his desk just as the second bell rang and the last of his twenty students filed into the room.

"Just because you are my nephew does not mean you can stroll in whenever you wish Gaige."

"What? Oh right, sorry", said a very out of breath Gaige Davies, "football ran late." He was Tyffani Patrick and Blair

Davies youngest son. He looked like his father aside from his coloring; he was tall and broad with dark hair, dark eyes and pale skin that tanned fairly well during the summer. Gaige was the first of his five nieces and nephews he would see that day, his oldest nephew Bryce would be the last.

"No worries. Next time just let me know okay."

"Yes sir," Gaige said taking his seat and catching his breath.

"Alright guys I hope you finished my favorite of Mr. Huxley's novels over the weekend because you have a pop quiz! I'll give you five minutes to study and no, I will not tell you what the questions are," Rylan said to a chorus of grumbling that would repeat itself five more times by the end of the day. He smiled to himself as his mind drifted to his wife at home in her own reverie.

She couldn't stand a dirty kitchen, wouldn't be able to sleep knowing there were dishes in the sink. Making short work of her chores, she headed off to bed. Passing the black and white photos of her family that lined the hallway to the bedrooms, she smiled broadly knowing she was helping it grow.

Their doctor would confirm it for them later that week and Teagan couldn't be more excited to see their "little bean" for the first time. She had known for a while that she was pregnant and told Rylan straight away. He was overjoyed at the news and was having more difficulty keeping it secret than Teagan was. Settling into bed after brushing her teeth, she fell asleep quickly and began to dream of the first time she met her husband.

Family

He stumbled out of the pub arm in arm with his brother Matthew, leaving the bartender laughing and waving their goodbyes to the few remaining stragglers. They had had what felt like all the whiskey in Ireland that night and were quite lucky they could still stand. Alcohol did not really affect Faeries as it did other beings. They required much more of it to reach their current state than would a human. They started on their second verse of "Oh Danny Boy" for probably the eighth time that night as they crested the hill and began their long journey home. Slightly blurred in the distance, Rylan could see two of the most striking women he had ever laid eyes on headed their way.

The bright colors of their dresses made their vivid scarlet hair even more so. The taller of the two wore her hair in a loose bun at the nape of her neck, her straight bangs soft and cut to just below her brow. The sleeves of her pale blue dress came to the middle of her toned biceps and fluttered slightly in the light breeze. It was cut low in front to reveal her ample bosom and cinched at her middle with a grey sash to show off her tiny waist. She gathered its length in her hands to ease the hike up the hill. The shorter of the two was built even more delicately than the first but, just as lovely. Her dress identical in fashion only hers was a rich plum with a white sash. She had one arm looped through her sisters' free arm; the other held her skirts just above her knee, the moonlight accentuating the porcelain that was their skin.

They were laughing with each other; sincere, hearty, familiar laughter. It was the most beautiful sound Rylan had heard yet in his 35 years. The brothers stopped at the top of the hill to steady themselves and catch their breath. Rylan was pleased to see the ladies would soon be within ear shot and he amused himself thinking he needed a decent spring fling. He had no idea that lovely, soft evening in March of 1914 would be one of the most important nights of his life.

"Lovely," Teagan whispered to Meagan, "don't make eye contact."

Meagan merely nodded and laughed her rich, throaty laugh in response.

"Excuse me lass," was barely intelligible through the slurred Irish brogue but, Rylan heard himself say it.

"You're excused sirs. Now if you don't mind, we're on our way home and don't need any trouble," Teagan said curtly as the girls continued past them.

"Great. Americans," Matthew said louder than he meant to, stopping the ladies in their tracks. Turning on their heels mid stride to face their inebriated counterparts, Meagan took the few steps necessary to close the distance between herself and Matthew. Placing her petite hands on her narrow hips, she began to give him a piece of her mind.

Oh boy, Teagan thought as she opened her wristlet to locate her cigarettes and matches. Rylan sidled over to Teagan as she finally got her match to strike and was relishing her first lung full of cherry vanilla Cavendish tobacco. Taking it from her hand Rylan took a long drag himself before handing it back to a surprised Teagan. Taking stock of the drunkard in front of her, she realized just how handsome he was.

He kept his tall frame lean with the construction work he did for his father's company, that same work gave his slightly sloped nose a fine dusting of freckles across his otherwise unblemished fair skin. He kept his blonde hair closely cropped because it was convenient and drew more attention to his cornflower blue eyes. He kept his heart guarded due to experience. *'Interesting,'* Teagan mused as she read him.

"What is?" Rylan asked. When all Teagan did was stare at him utterly shocked that he had heard her, he introduced himself.

"My name is Rylan, Rylan McCarthy. That poor sod getting the mickey taken out of him is my brother Matthew. And who might you be?"

"Teagan. Patrick. Teagan Patrick," she stuttered, still shaken that he could hear her thoughts.

"Pleased to meet you Miss Patrick," he said taking her hand and grazing it softly with his lips.

"Likewise. That little spit fire berating your idiot brother is my little sister, Meagan." She pronounced her little sister's name just like her own but, with an 'M' instead of a 'T'.

Lacing his fingers through hers, he took another drag from the cigarette she still held in her other hand.

"Aye and she's doing a fine job of it too! Has she much practice?" he inquired. Smoke escaped his full lips as he chuckled in his brother's direction.

"She does. She's quite the temper, rivals my own," she said exhaling the last of the smoke in her lungs.

"Is that so?"

"Aye. 'Tis. I've a good sense of humor and am quick to laugh but, push the right button and it's a black mood you'll leave with."

"If I were to push the right button it should do the opposite no? Still screaming involved but, more fun for everyone," he added winking.

"Excuse me Mr. McCarthy but, you really don't know me well enough to be concerned with my buttons."

"Whose fault is that then?"

"We've only just met so I'm not quite sure who would be at fault yet."

"It isn't as though I'm not trying Ms. Patrick. I'm inclined to blame you."

"Are you now? Well, too bad for you I'm a pure and a virtuous woman. It will take more than pretty words to undo my buttons sir."

She laughed inwardly at her lie, what he didn't know wouldn't hurt him.

"Very well, I'll certainly keep that in mind Ms. Patrick."

"Please do, Mr. McCarthy."

"Ah it looks like she's done! She's giving him her card sure."

Sure enough Meagan offered her hand, curtseyed and walked toward Rylan and her sister smiling broadly.

"So it would seem. Good talk McCarthy. We'll be seeing each other again I'm sure," she let go of his hand and gave him their almost finished cigarette. He nodded at her in reply and stuck the end between his teeth.

Looping her arm through her sisters they continued making their way home, leaving two perplexed-looking Fae in their wake.

Matthew and Rylan McCarthy came to call the very next day.

Teagan turned over in her sleep as she felt Rylan reminiscing with her, smiling to himself.

It was finally lunch time and Rylan was grateful for the hour-long respite from the angst and neurosis that accompanied young adulthood. He made his way down the street to Jack's Bistro where his favorite lunch was served up by one of his family's dearest friends. The bell clanged when he opened the door indicating a new customer had arrived and the proprietor of the establishment rounded the corner carrying a tray full of pumpkin chocolate chip scones. Jack Anthony was tall and lean. He kept his short, dyed platinum blonde hair cut in a Mohawk and thick black framed glasses accentuated his dark brown eyes perfectly. Jack had known Teagan for most of their lives, they had met in Tombstone while Rylan was at war, and they had become fast friends. Jack grinned widely at him, setting down his tray as he strode toward the counter to greet him.

"If it isn't my favorite fellow Blonde," he said wiping chocolate dust from his hands onto his black apron so he could give Rylan a hug without soiling his shirt.

"It is indeed! How are you today friend?"

"Oh, business as usual," Jack replied as they let go their embrace and set into their usual banter.

"That is excellent to hear! I'm glad I beat the lunch rush. I'm bloody starved."

"Now I know that's not true. I taught your wife how to cook and she does a damned fine job of it."

"This is very true but, breakfast seems ages ago!"

"Lucky for you the brussel sprouts chips have just come out of the oven and I happen to know how you take your tea. Sit, and I'll have you taken care of."

"Ah you are a saint among men. Can I also have one of your famous club sandwiches? And water today instead of tea please."

"Of course! How do you feel about poppy seed ciabatta and prosciutto instead of bacon?"

"I feel like you should start making that ASAP and that sounds amazing."

Rylan finished his fare just as the rush was starting. Jack gave him a dozen fresh scones to take home to his wife, a half dozen to give his coworkers and was quickly back running his kitchen. Rylan checked in with Teagan mentally and found her still dreaming blissfully.

"So, who are these young men you two are spending so much of your time getting ready for," Timothy Patrick asked from the doorway of the room his daughters shared. He did not wish to invade the flurry of mess and activity in front of him; dresses and undergarments strewn about, his daughters jockeying for position in front of the vanity. Meagan nearly tripped as she held a red satin confection in front of her to inspect it. Teagan turned to look and shook her head in disgust.

"Matthew and Rylan McCarthy," she responded knowing full well that her father was aware who they were. Mother had told him, of course, as he hadn't been there the day before when they came to call. Finishing her kohl liner and mascara, she turned to help Meagan into the dove grey dress she had finally decided on.

When she was finished, she stooped to clean up the mess her sister created while that youngest of Patrick children set about applying her own make up.

"Ah I see. These wouldn't be Bryan McCarthy's boys would they," he looked concerned, "Bryan and I came up together and if his sons are anything like their father, I will not expect you home before dawn."

At this he strode into the now partially clean room. Stopping Teagan mid task and turning her around, he retied the black ribbon at the back of her pale pink dress.

"This dress is very low-cut daughter, in the front and the back. No, I certainly won't be expecting you home before dawn if you insist on going out like this," he said frowning as he finished his knot. She rolled her eyes in answer.

"Father, Teagan and Rylan are our chaperones. I am certain they will ensure we behave and that my honor remains intact," Meagan reassured the Patrick Patriarch with a small smile.

"Well, I just don't want another incident like Mumbai. Charles has only just begun speaking to me again," he said nearly pouting, a rather amusing expression on their centuries old father's face.

"Well, let that be a lesson to you never to let your teenaged daughters loose on their own in India to 'chase the dragon.' Especially when your friend's handsome sons are their tour guides," Teagan managed to get out without breaking into a fit of laughter.

As she slept soundly, this pleasant memory bled into another she was rather fond of.

Sporting stick on mustaches, the girls dressed in the blouses and knee pants they used for riding horseback as well as long coats to guard against the weather. They braided their hair as neatly as possible, tucking it under their top hats to appear less conspicuous as the tavern, 'Molly Bloom's', they were going to didn't exactly allow women, especially not American women. Rylan opened the service entrance door, and they were instantly enveloped in a haze of smoke, laughter and debauchery that typically accompanies copious amounts of alcohol. "Somebody's Sweetheart I Want to be" was being played on a slightly out of tune piano from the corner of the bar. Meagan and Teagan doffed their coats and gloves before the group made their way to the bar, trying to blend in as well as possible.

"She seems quite smitten with him, no," Rylan observed Meagan's hand brushing Matthew's as they crossed the room.

"Does it matter really? We are only here for another two weeks."

"No, I suppose it does not. For what it's worth, I have thoroughly enjoyed my month of chaperone duty," he added winking roguishly at her.

"Of this I have no doubt but, as I have said before; we are partners in chaperone duty only," Teagan firmly reminded him as she silently wished it to be true and hearing Rylan wished it weren't.

"Ah, poker again fellas? Ready for me to make your wives angry at the money you're about to lose," Teagan grinned mockingly and stroked her faux mustache as they approached the card table.

A diminutive man to her right with a grey beard and ruddy cheeks handed her a cigar as she pulled out and sat in the chair next to his.

"Not tonight, Rylan's bought in for the pair of ya and he's the best hand this side of Kerry sure," he said, eyes twinkling. Her jaw dropped as Rylan set a large whiskey in front of her and winked as he took the empty chair across from hers. He could see her blush through the cigar smoke between them. He swallowed a large mouthful of whiskey hoping to calm the furious tattoo his heart was beating against his chest. Dropping his gaze to the table he began to arrange his chips in front of him, hoping she would not notice how nervous she made him.

"Where the River Shannon Flows," started up as Meagan and Matt started their second whiskey. They had come to 'Molly's' at least once a week since they had begun courting officially three weeks ago. The McCarthy's uncle owned the club, and their cousins were bartenders; thus, the reason they were comfortable sneaking the girls in. She was surprised at how quickly she had fallen for him. He was handsome yes but, she was not a shallow girl. He was charming of course but she was not easily seduced. It was his humor that had won her over. She was so serious herself and the only other person to make her laugh as Matt did was Teagan. Teagan, who was currently listening to her as evidenced by the smile on her sisters faux mustachioed face as she nodded knowingly in Meagan's direction.

"What are you thinking about to make you smile so, my

love," Matt asked her gently. "You," she drained the last of her drink, "always you. Let's dance."

Taking her hand, he led her to the dance floor. Across the room a very intoxicated man protested the sight of "two men" dancing together with a loud guffaw and a hard slam of his glass on the table. Nearly breaking the crystal, he stood up and made toward the couple but was quickly escorted from the club. Refusing to let the disturbance ruin their good mood, Meagan and Matthew laughed heartily as the well lubricated pianist struck up a slightly off-key version of "The Skye Boat Song."

She wished she had Teagan's gift so she could know what Matt was thinking.

She knew how draining it could be and had never before wished it in her life but, her desire for reassurance was reaching a nearly overwhelming level; she dared not ask Matthew for reassurance, lest she appear needy. She laid her head against his chest as he spun her about the floor. She felt safe. She felt like she was home. There amidst the cigar smoke and booze-fueled good natured insults, she felt herself consumed by happiness. It was as though she had been dipped in a sea of sunshine; always warm and never burned. She only wished Matthew would let her know he felt the same.

As the night rushed toward dawn, the only two still conscious players at the poker table were the chaperones.

Joseph, the dealer and only sober soul in the pub, was ready to throw in the towel and told the pair as much as he dealt their last hand. Matthew helped Eamon and Seamus, the bartending cousins, clean up shop as they all joined in singing "That's An Irish Lullaby." Teagan and Rylan sat across from one another, each refusing to show the other their hand; the drink adding fuel to their already competitive natures.

"Call," Rylan said raising a pale brow.

"Royal Flush," Teagan said smiling like the cat that ate the canary, her top hat askew on her scarlet crown.

"Damn," and draining the rest of his glass were Rylan's only reply.

"Well, well, well," Joseph said around the cigar in his teeth, "looks as though someone has met his match."

"Oh, he will never admit to that," Teagan said stubbing out her own cigar and stretching her back before slowly rising from her chair, remembering to fix her hat as she did.

Leaving Rylan to sulk, she turned to find Meagan helping Matt and the bar tenders clean. This was a night for the ages indeed if her messiest of siblings was inspired to tidy up.

"You ready to go little one? It's almost four o'clock, father will start to worry soon." Meagan only nodded in answer, too absorbed in letting the rag distract her from her feelings to really hear her sister. Looking back at Rylan she asked, "You coming chaperone or, are you going to sit there and lick your wounds?" Rylan nodded curtly and headed toward the back where they had left their outerwear.

"Thank you for putting up with us," she called to the remaining staff, "I know we can be a handful."

"Anything for a gorgeous woman darlin," Seamus slurred at her, "double that for two gorgeous red heads."

She blushed suddenly realizing they had known their secret the whole time and turning to leave she noted that her charge had already gone. Rylan grabbed her around the waist and pulled her into a tight hug as she rounded the corner. She began to protest his proximity but was silenced by his mouth on hers. He kissed her gently and moved his left hand from her waist to her face, grazing her cheek bone lightly with his fingers. He kissed her again more deeply. Drawing her closer to him, he parted her lips with the tip of his tongue, and she dug her fingers into his hair; turning his head left as she turned right and slid her tongue over his. His hand moved from her cheek down to her collar bone and then to the buttons on her blouse. Gently massaging his tongue with hers, she placed her hand in the one that was moving to places it shouldn't and whispered, "We cannot."

He laced his fingers in hers and gently replied "why not?" Before kissing her again and twining her scarlet locks between the fingers of his free hand. When she did not answer, he gently bit her bottom lip and moved her against the wall behind her. He pulled back and asked again "why not?" Pressing against her, placed another passionate kiss on her full lips. Her mind was racing. She could not think straight with his thoughts in her head and his tongue in her mouth.

"Where did this come from all of a sudden? Usually, you keep me at arm's length and now we're kissing in the back of a pub?"

Then she heard it. Between his thoughts of how she smelled, how she tasted and how she would taste; *I love you.*

'Teagan I am in love with you,' Rylan thought desperately, *'I am done pretending otherwise.'*

She pushed him away roughly and gasped "I hear you," swallowing her pride and fear, "I can hear you."

He breathed deeply, his eyes now staring at the ground

that was now between them. He took her hands in his, "all the time?"

"I hear you often. Not every thought, I try to block most of you out but, you are quite persistent." She could see the worry on his face and feel it in her bones.

"Is that why you won't be with me? I am too persistent? Or is it that I push you away," he asked still refusing to look at her, like a child being scolded, "I only push you away because I have feelings and am not good enough to inflict them upon you."

She took his face in her hands and looked into his bright blue eyes, "Inflict? No. You are a good man Rylan and certainly good enough for me. I would not be with you because you are admittedly a playboy and I have no desire to be your 'Spring Fling'."

"Ah, you heard that, did you?"

"How could I not? It was the only thing you could think of every time you saw me that first week our siblings began courting."

"Well, you are rather lovely darling."

"And I do not wish to be had just because of the way I look."

"You deserve more than that and I didn't know I could ever want more than that."

"I know. You have never let yourself want more than that Rylan."

"No, I haven't. It's easier just to have relations and go my own way."

"You're not convincing me I was wrong to refuse you."

"Teagan you have my heart. Fractured and flawed though

it may be, it is yours. You have captured it and I do not want it back," he looked up at her his voice soft and vulnerable.

She let her guards down and was flooded with emotion.

Love, loathing, doubt, respect, admiration and lust overwhelmed her all at once. Love was the strongest though it was closely followed by lust. Rylan was consumed by it; he was sick with it; it coursed through his body along with the blood in his veins. He felt suffocated and revived by it at once. He wanted her and wanted her to want him; he wanted her to love him back. Teagan was paralyzed, relieved, and invigorated by the rush of it all; she leaned into their fear and made the smartest bet she ever would, though she wouldn't know that for years afterward.

"Teagan, I love you."

"Yes," she said before kissing him, "I can feel that."

She pulled him gently to her and kissed his throat. She put her arms around his neck and her mouth on his mouth, sliding her tongue between their lips. When she pulled back to take a breath, he made quick work of their clothing and good use of the barrels full of whiskey that stood waiting to be consumed.

Teagan stirred gently as she became aware her husband was on his way home. Opening her eyes to midafternoon sunlight, she smiled knowing she was the luckiest girl in the world and happy to be so loved. She slowly finished waking up and began to ready herself for what would no doubt be an entertaining evening. Taking her under garments from their respective drawers in the dresser, choosing a white V-neck long sleeved t-shirt and her favorite pair of jeans from the closet she dressed quickly and headed to the bathroom to take care of her other needs.

She had just started braiding her persistently curly hair when she heard Rylan come through the front door. Tying off the bottom of her braid, she plugged in her flat iron so she could straighten her almost too long bangs.

'It's time for a trim,' she thought.

"Yes, you are looking rather unkempt my love," Rylan chuckled behind her, "I suppose I will just have to love you in spite of it."

"Oh, whatever would I do without you," she rolled her eyes at him.

"Be bored," he said sitting on the sink in front of her.

"I would find ways to amuse myself, I'm sure. You aren't as interesting as you think you are," she winked at him as she finished her hair.

"I whole heartedly disagree ma'am, are you almost ready?"

"Ready as I'll ever be." She leaned forward and hugged him hard enough to pull him off the counter. Placing a kiss on her forehead as he set him down, he took her hand and lead her out of the room.

"Do I smell pastries?"

"Good God you are pregnant. Jack sent home some scones for you."

Teagan opened the black bakery box and took a chocolate raspberry one to go as they left for dinner with their family.

Next of Kin

They reached the manor house a full fifteen minutes before everyone else and happily assisted Rose Patrick, Teagan's mother, finish up dinner preparations. Rylan and Timothy, Teagan's father, The Faerie King of Bansalee, chatted idly as they set the table. Teagan hummed 'green sleeves' with her mother as they finished dishing food into their formal dishware.

'*Uh oh*' Teagan thought breathing through her mouth, '*Salmon.*'

"Mom, I'll be right back," barely choking back her vomit as she ran to the bathroom. She dry heaved over the cool porcelain after she had emptied the little that was in her stomach and cursed her nausea for making an appearance at such an inopportune time. She had no idea how she would hide this from them. The salmon would be set out on the table and was one of her favorite dishes. How would she deflect it without drawing suspicion?

"Teagan," came her mother's gentle knock at the door.

"Yeah ma, I'll be right out," breathing deeply to steady her stomach.

"Let me in," she knocked more insistently.

Rising slowly on shaky knees, she opened the door sheepishly, allowing her mother a wide berth as she entered the bathroom.

"How far along are you?"

"We find out for sure this week. Please don't tell anyone, we aren't quite ready yet," she plead feeling like she was fifteen again asking her mother to keep poor marks from her father.

"Very well, what shall we serve for dinner then," she asked, wetting a washcloth, and pressing to her daughter's forehead.

"Cheeseburgers, bacon cheeseburgers," suddenly ravenous, Teagan's stomach growled audibly, "And sweet potato fries," she added licking her lips.

"We better get started, we'll tell everyone the fish was bad," her mother winked at her, kissing her cheek before heading back to the kitchen.

Rinsing her mouth out and washing her face before following her mother, Teagan again was amazed at how lucky she was and choked back happy tears.

"Change of plans," she heard her mother calling to her father, "you get to break in your new grill darling!"

The rest of her siblings and their spouses trickled in slowly. Hugging each other in welcome as each family member arrived. Meagan and Matt were last as usual and got there at about six, just as the sun was beginning to set. Due to the change of fare most of the male family members were in the back yard, keeping a close watch on the hamburgers, stomachs grumbling.

"Ugh my last client today was absolutely beastly," Meagan scowled shaking her red curls free of her green wool beanie and taking off her brown leather boots.

"Oh yeah? Mine too," Tyffani asked, pouring her youngest sister a glass of red wine, "tell me everything."

"He was just in the worst mood," she began, taking a grateful sip from her glass, "his energy was disgusting and the stress knots in his shoulders? I will never understand why humans insist upon doing everything inside, sitting at desks."

"Anytime you want to help wash and cut these sweet potatoes, I won't be upset about it," Teagan directed at her gossiping sisters.

"Mine just droned on and on about how he 'just realized his mother has ruined every relationship he's ever had'," Tyffani continued, completely ignoring Teagan's request. Tyffani Patrick Davies was the eldest child and almost a spitting image of their mother, raven curls down to her tiny waist, full mouth, and slightly sloped nose. Her dark blue eyes were one of the few minor variances between the Patrick Matriarch and her eldest child.

The oldest and youngest Patrick children clinked glasses in cheers and made their way through the spacious kitchen and living room to the back yard.

"I tell ya ma, I just can't get no respect 'round here," Teagan joked.

"That's just kids sometimes," Rose shook her head, "you better get used to it doll."

They finished their dinner prep singing their favorite songs at each other and headed out to join the rest of their family. Her brothers were heading in to set the table as she and their mother were headed outside.

"Don't worry ladies, we'll handle the kitchen properly," Travis teased as they passed each other.

"Yeah right," Teagan rolled her eyes at him shaking her head as Seth laughed at them both.

"Don't forget napkins please," Rose called after them.

"Aye ma," they responded in unison. Travis was second oldest and had their mother's face, jet black hair and big brown eyes. He had his father's build, tall and lean, and his grandfather's fiery temper. In the way of appearance, Seth was the "black sheep" of the family. He was only a few inches taller than Teagan and wiry as scarecrow. His white hair had always been unruly, making him appear more eccentric than he actually was, and his violet eyes were always alight with excitement at some new technological advancement he had discovered.

"Are those burgers almost ready Da? It's like we sprung this on you last minute or, something," she teased her father as she approached him at the grill and hugged him around the waist.

"Almost ready my little pixie," he said kissing her on the forehead, "do me a favor and grab me a smoke will you?"

Teagan turned to Sadee and yelled, "Oi! Blondie, grab dad a cigar, will you?"

In the middle of a conversation with Jonna, their sister-in-law, she shot her sister a dark look and went to the walk-in humidor as she requested. Laughing at his children, Timothy Patrick shook his head and went back to tending their food. Standing on tip toes to kiss her father's cheek, Teagan left to join Jonna and Rylee near the Koi Pond where they sat deep in conversation. Her mother took her place next to her father while he finished up grilling their main dish. Tyffani and Meagan, who were sitting at the elaborate outdoor bar talking animatedly with their husbands Blair and Matt, waved hello as Teagan passed them on her way to her other sisters.

She only nodded in return, taking a deep breath to stave off another wave of nausea.

Taking off her socks and rolling up her jeans, she put her feet in the cool water and lay her head in Rylee's lap, listening to their discussion.

"It was so disheartening," Rylee continued, starting to unbraid Teagan's hair, "Sadee and I worked on him for thirty minutes but, the poor little guy just wasn't strong enough. His lungs refused to cooperate."

"Oh, that's awful," Jonna shook her head, taking a sip from her wine glass, "I don't know how you guys do it day in and day out. I would be a wreck!"

"It's the toughest job you'll ever love," the twins said in unison as Sadee returned, taking her seat next to Jonna. Giggling and raising their glasses, they all finished off their wine and exhaled contentedly. Sadee was a nurse in the Emergency Room and Rylee a nurse in Pediatrics at Bansail Hospital, which was established almost a thousand years before they were a twinkle in their father's eye, by their great grandfather. Rylee and Sadee were between Seth and Teagan in age.

Much like Teagan and Meagan, they were an interesting mix of Patrick and Hagan family traits. They were average height and delicately built. Rylee kept her straight dark blond hair shoulder length; Sadee preferred hers in a pixie cut, highlighted with platinum streaks. They got their large almond shaped blue eyes from their grandmother Patrick, as did Tyffani.

"So, Teagan, how has work been for you," Jonna inquired.

"Same stuff, different day," she gave her usual answer, "I want to hear about what you've got going at the studio. Mother said it's very good."

Her sister-in-law's deep brown eyes lit up as she set into her description of the new art that would be arriving.

Jonna was a curator at La Rose Gallery; an art studio Teagan's Grandmother La Rose started in 1882, the year before she died. Jonna met Seth while they were at college. They had married after dating for nearly a decade and were very content not having children, much to Rose Patrick's chagrin. Jonna was very even tempered and almost always had a smile playing at her naturally red lips. She had long, straight black hair and brown eyes that reflected her Korean heritage. Her skin tanned easily, inciting no small amount of jealousy from her sisters-in-law. She was the same height as her husband and just as thin. They were adorable together and Teagan loved that she made her brother so happy; Jonna was very easy to be around, and Teagan loved that too.

She closed her eyes and listened passively as Rylee massaged her head, her curls freed from their short-lived braid.

"Girls, supper's on," their mother called to them as Jonna was describing a very adult sculpture that would soon be displayed.

Bullet dodged and completely sated; Teagan helped her sisters clean up the kitchen when everyone had had their fill. The men folk, brothers in law included, went outside for a post dinner cigar and scotch. The Patrick's had been blessed with seven children: two boys, five girls. This meant that Timothy Patrick was gifted Sons in Law and for that he was grateful. Growing up in a big family was the most fun Teagan had ever been privy to and couldn't imagine life any other way. She couldn't wait to have a small brood of her own, four, that's what she and Rylan had decided on. He hoped karma wouldn't curse him with girls and Teagan wished for three boys and one girl.

Rylan would be an amazing father and she thought he would just be too cute with a little daddy's girl to spoil.

Tyffani and Meagan were at their usual chore of clearing the table of dishes. Teagan washed, her mother dried; the twins, Rylee and Sadee, cleaned the stove and counter tops. Her sisters finished their chores first and headed out back to commiserate with their male counterparts. Teagan stayed behind helping her mother dry and put away the few remaining dishes.

"I am so excited to be a grandmother again," Rose smiled, eyes misting with joy; she rested her hand on her second youngest daughters' belly and closed her eyes letting a tear drop from her long, dark lashes.

"The nausea will soon pass and then you will be hungry all day long," she added chuckling. Taking Teagan's hand, her mother led them outside to where the rest of their family waited.

"Finally," Travis snapped exasperatedly as Teagan and their mother exited the sliding glass door onto the back patio of their family's stately home. She made her way slowly through the plethora of siblings before her, to her husband's side.

"Anyone for a game of Schwoozle," Rylee challenged raising a blond eyebrow at Tyffani.

"You're on," she responded, an ornery grin lighting up her face.

"Good," Sadee said, "let's pick teams!"

"Please," Meagan interjected rolling her eyes, "the teams are always the same."

"They really are," Travis shook his head at his sisters, "let's mix it up a bit."

"Agreed brother," Seth nodded to Travis, "how about boys against girls this time? Only, I want Teagan on my team!" He declared, pulling his sister to him by the hand.

"Ugh, everyone always wants Teagan on their team," Matt grumbled.

"Duh," Meagan laughed, "Tea always wins."

"I win when you aren't making up your own rules little sister," she mock scolded Meagan.

"Oh, I don't know that Teagan should join this round," Rylan added narrowing his eyes at his wife.

"Fine, no absinthe for you then," Blair Davies laughed heartily at his brother in law's protest and raised his green liquid filled glass in Teagan's direction.

"Well," Teagan began haughtily, "seeing as I don't have the proper parts to be on the boys' team and we have those of the female persuasion in abundance, I think I will sit this one out. We could use a referee anyways."

Kissing her husband's hand, she took a softly cushioned chair to her father's right and settled in to watch the mayhem that was her family's go-to pastime.

Timothy Patrick took his daughters' hand in his and kissed the back of it gently. Teagan heard what he was preparing to tell her, and she rolled her eyes inwardly at her mother's inability to keep anything secret from the King.

"I am so excited for you babog and I am glad to be a

grandfather again," his deep voice began gently, "Rylan will be a wonderful father."

He said no more on the matter, only sat back and watched his children play; interrupting only once to break up a fist fight between his sons over who would be captain.

After much deliberation, Seth ended up captain of the yellow team and chose for his team mates; his brother and brothers-in-law. Tyffani was chosen as leader of the green team and took her sisters and her sister-in-law, Jonna, as her team. He did want boys vs. girls after all. It was a rousing game as usual, and Teagan had to threaten bodily harm more than once on both sides to discourage cheating. This would be the only time Seth encouraged a battle of the sexes as The Green team won by 30 points; leaving their male halves with belly's full of absinthe and their wives responsible for getting them home safely. Collecting their belongings, the Patrick children and their respective spouses began the slow process of leaving their parents' home.

"Come now siblings, let's leave our old mother and father to bed," an exhausted Teagan directed at her drunken brothers, "it is way past their bedtime after all."

"Oh yes," Seth slurred slightly, "we wouldn't want father to miss a wink of his beauty sleep."

"Who said anything about sleeping," their father grinned as he lifted his wife in a bear hug.

"And I'm going to puke in my mouth," Sadee faked vomiting into a trash can, causing Teagan to breathe deeply to prevent sympathetic emesis. They finished hugging and kissing their parents' goodbye; giggling like school children as they usually did after departing their weekly family dinners.

The twins left first, as their shared apartment was farthest away. The remaining couples left as their conversations wound down. Taking Rylan's hand in hers, Teagan and her husband left last; they headed southward, Teagan grateful for the cool night air that engulfed them as they traveled swiftly home.

Work

Arriving to work with her usual promptness and feeling very energized, Teagan made her way down the drab hallway to her office. Clearly men had decided on the décor for the police building and nary a one had any taste. Jack had had a field day in here.

"Dear god, it's like the seventies threw up in here after a bad acid trip," he had said. She was remembering his fitted t-shirt and jeans self, clucking disapproval at the beige color on the walls of her office; immediately insisting on a peacock blue instead with a dark grey Berber carpet in place of the lime green tile. Deciding on Jack's Bistro for lunch she found herself at the stained black wood office door that her dear friend had helped her choose. She unlocked it and entered her little sanctuary amidst the madness that was her daily grind; her own anise and myrrh noted perfume had permeated the space over the years and greeted her when she opened the door. Placing her mug of hot chocolate and one of the pumpkin cherry scones Jack had sent home yesterday on the white birch wood desk, she removed her gloves and tucked them into the pockets of her outerwear. She unwound the mustard yellow scarf from around her neck and hung it along with her dove grey hooded peacoat on the polished copper coat rack that stood near the door.

Tuesday was the day the brass had deemed appropriate for meetings so, Teagan dressed a little more business and less casual than she would on her normal workday. She wore her hair straight and let its length fall freely down her back. The vivid color contrasted beautifully with the turquoise of the cuffed long line blouse she had tucked neatly into her black high-waisted trousers. She took advantage of still being able to wear heels and had chosen an unnecessarily tall pair of black leather boots. She was sure she would be regretting them around 15:00 but, it wouldn't be much longer before a full pregnant belly would cause an extra six inches to throw her off balance.

She beamed at the thought of it.

She sipped her beverage carefully and sat down a moment to review her notes from two nights before. She printed what she had and put it in a new file folder with a new case number. She liked file folders. They kept her organized and made it easy to keep track of cases whether she or, someone else needed to review them.

Satisfied that she was prepared for her meeting, she gathered her things, locked her office door behind her and made her way to the conference room where several of her coworkers were already settling in. The division Lieutenant and Captain had not yet arrived and probably wouldn't until five minutes after the meeting was supposed to have started, which meant Teagan had a good 15-minute wait.

Her stomach grumbled audibly and the Sergeant sitting

nearest the door she had just entered gave her a concerned look.

"Did you eat breakfast McCarthy?"

"Aye sir I did, though apparently my body disagrees."

"Hopefully this meeting will be a short one then and we can all go to an early lunch," the portly Sergeant patted the substantial middle his dark grey uniform shirt was struggling to keep covered.

"Indeed," she nodded agreement and chose a comfortable looking chair at the end of a table toward the back of the room. Just when she got situated, her least favorite coworker made his entrance. Benjamin Smith had developed a crush on Teagan when they were in the academy together and had never gotten over it. He was tall and lean. He kept his thinning mouse brown hair cut as close to his scalp as was possible without shaving it all off and his dishwater grey eyes were always far too eager for attention. He had just been promoted to detective and would be put through his paces over the next six months of training for that. Just as she dreaded, he had spotted her and was making a bee line for the empty chair to her right. Sergeant Thaumes, pronounced 'Thomas,' who was in charge of detectives and who was also her favorite sergeant had snuck in quietly and took the seat to her left.

"Good lord," he lamented under his breath, "I am not looking forward to him being in my unit."

"Nor am I," a startled Teagan whispered out of the side of her mouth.

Sergeant Jacob Thaumes was one of the tallest faeries she knew, nearly six and a half feet tall and naturally well-muscled, owing to the fact that his paternal grandfather had been an elf. He was fair skinned, had beautiful amber eyes and, black hair that most of the human women they worked with were envious of. He kept it cut short like most of the male officers Teagan worked with chose to do but, he had let it grow to shoulder length once upon a time. He had been a Ranger employed by her Uncle, her mother's brother, and King of The Sulach Court in Northern Arizona. He had joined the police department when he and his wife had started their family; he wanted to be closer to home and to travel less. He was an exceptional recruit, had been chosen for the TAC Team right out of the academy and had been appointed a detective when Teagan was still just a patrol officer. He had hand-picked her for his squad when he had been promoted to the position of Detective Sergeant. That was five years ago this April and neither of them had regretted the decision once. This was no mean feat as young Teagan McCarthy had been quite the insubordinate patrol officer. She was smarter than most of her coworkers and their superiors and she knew it; her problem was knowing how to control her mouth. It had taken her a good six years on the street and no small amount of written reprimands before she settled down and learned to choose her battles.

"Where is my hot chocolate by the way?" her sergeant teased, "worst detective ever."

"Hey McCarthy," Benjamin Smith winked as he settled in next to her.

"Hello Detective Smith," she said flatly.

"Is that a new blouse?"

"Can I help you?"

"You wear it very well."

"No, it is not a new blouse and I am still married," she fired back; rolling her eyes and flashing the ring finger of her left hand at him so he could see the druidic rune for 'wholeness' tattooed in black ink.

It was the rune Fae used in their wedding ceremonies, as rings weren't used to signify marriage among them. She had the rune for 'warrior' on the index finger of her right hand and the rune for fertility on her right thumb, both in white ink.

"That is a shame."

"I'm sure my husband would disagree."

The last of the sergeants and detectives had found suitable places to sit for the next hour, or so Teagan hoped, and the Captain and Lieutenant finally made their appearance. Ah right on time. They were five minutes earlier than anyone expected them to be and all present were glad to be witness to this most likely one-time occurrence. Lieutenant Bashward entered the room first, Captain Mizner right on his heels. The LT, as he was affectionately called by his subordinates, was a short, stocky old man with greying hair, parchment yellow skin and pea green eyes. Rumors ran rampant that he was part dwarf but Teagan knew better than to put any stock in the rumor mill and besides, his beard wasn't nearly epic enough to indicate dwarf hood. He always dressed in full uniform and today was no exception, dark grey long-sleeved shirt and trousers with all the stripes and pins in perfect order.

His duty belt, always meticulously kept, and his black boots shined to a mirror ball level of gleam. The Captain was a full head taller than the Lieutenant but, still two inches shorter than Teagan's own 5 and a half feet. He had dark auburn hair, chestnut brown eyes and perfectly tanned skin. He had chosen business casual attire for today's meeting as he usually did; black long-sleeved button down tucked into grey tweed trousers and black loafers that hadn't been paid nearly the amount of attention the LT's boots had gotten. The only weapon he carried on his belt was one of the guns Seth had custom made for the department. Since faeries are allergic to iron, it's lethal in fact; he developed a vanadium and graphite version of Teagan's favorite German made 45 caliber semi-automatic handgun. It had become part of their required equipment in recent years due to so many humans having and using them. Because they are supernatural beings, Faeries have many more choices for de-escalation than human

police but, it's always better to have a tool and not need it than need it and not have it.

"Good morning," LT began, "I know it is a bit early for a meeting but, thank you all for your promptness. We won't delay you anymore than necessary, we know you all have business to attend to. Now, we'll start by reviewing a call Squad 4 took last week. It was a bit of glamour gone awry, resulting with a barking chicken and a very irate human neighbor."

Teagan stifled a laugh before zoning out the LT's monotone voice. He wouldn't get to the detectives for a while. She let her mind wander a bit; going through the various afternoon tasks she needed to take care of.

Questioning the Elf Knight Orion was at the top of the list. Her stomach grumbled again though less audibly this time and she decided that food was at the top of the list, Orion could be second. She knew that by the time she got around to him, he would be in the park guarding Queen

Khora while she and the rest of her minions took tea. She loved feeding the ducks at the pond while surveying the children for suitable changelings. She was as disgusting a Winter Queen as any there ever had been and she was drawing out the mourning period for her daughter, The Empress Tylane, as long as she could; The Empress had been exiled years before Teagan was born, and no one had seen hide nor hair since. She, along with the rest of the Folk she knew, was sure one hundred forty-six years was quite long enough to mourn a traitor; too long if you asked anyone with sense. Who the hell would want to dress entirely in black for that amount of time anyway? Clearly fashion sense wasn't the only faculty of The Queen's that was going. It had long been rumored that she was mad and not in the usual Winter Queen way. She had supposedly taken to drinking the blood of changelings and using their bodies for firewood. It was bad enough to take human children from their homes and replace them with faeries that would torture human adults at length but, to brutalize them for one's own amusement was just heinous.

"Teagan are you still awake back there," the gravelly voice of her Captain cut through her reverie like a broadsword through a sapling.

"Aye sir," she cleared her throat, "just thinking of ways to help prevent under aged drinking. You're correct in saying human issues affect us all sir." She was glad she could multitask and had recovered with rather a smooth lie.

"Thank you, Detective McCarthy," he smiled politely back at her, "what progress have you made on the Collins' homicide from Sunday?"

"I have a short list of suspects. One of which I plan

to question today. His answers will most likely lead to the second suspect sir."

"Very well then, good work detective. Let your sergeant know if you need any assistance, I'm sure the newest addition to your department could benefit from seeing a seasoned vet in action."

"I'll keep that in mind sir," she feigned enthusiasm and hoped it wasn't as obviously fake as it felt. The last division to report was The TAC Team. The Tactics Annihilation and Containment team was full of former Marines who were still gung-ho and loved to blow things up. They happened to be some of the most intelligent men she worked with as well. There were only ten of them and it was very much a 'he man woman haters club.' They oozed testosterone and any time they weren't on a call out, they busied themselves by working out and running drills. It was intense but it kept them on point and intensity was required if you wanted to be part of their specialty unit. They took their job very seriously and Teagan loved them like brothers. Their Sergeant, Murphy, was giving The Captain his analysis of The Borderlands crime scene and every male in the room was eating it up. Most of them lived vicariously through the TAC Team's unusual calls. Galen Murphy was one of Teagan's favorite coworkers.

He stood just under six feet, kept himself fit and almost always had a smile on his handsome face. His skin was lighter than Teagan's own alabaster hue, his pale blonde hair rivaled her husband's, and his large dark brown eyes were always clear and full of mischief. He and Rylan had worked closely with Michael Collins during the uprising, they joined the Royal English Force afterward and had remained friends ever since.

He had explained to Teagan what is now known as PTSD but, then was called 'Shell Shock.' Rylan had come home from war with an awful case of it and neither of them knew exactly how to handle it. Galen was no stranger to the horrors they had seen and knew how to deal with the stress it put on him and his fellow soldiers. He helped The McCarthy's through many bad nights, and they were forever grateful to him. She was sure Rylan wanted him to be their son's god father but, would let him ask Len himself.

"Nice lie back there McCarthy," Len chortled as they exited their meeting and headed outside to go to lunch.

"I take under aged drinking very seriously sir and so should you. Fine Irish Whiskey should only rot the livers of professional booze hounds like you and I."

"Indeed. Though from what your husband let slip, you won't be having your share of the drink much for the next year or, so," he grinned broadly at her.

"Oh, he finally told you," she nearly squealed with delight. She grabbed him to her in a tight hug that garnered more than a few curious stares from their coworkers.

"He did woman, will you let me breathe. By The Oracle your strength has kept in your old age."

"Old? Please, I am in my prime. 121 is the perfect age."

"If you say so, Princess. Can I take you to lunch?"

"Jack's Bistro?"

"Hell yes. He makes the best sandwiches in town."

"Then, yes. I want to swing by the studio and see if Olive will go too if that's alright?"

"Olive? Sure. She's decent enough."

"I don't know that she's been decent a day in her life but, she's good Folk none the less."

"Fair enough, I would like to go with you to question Orion later as well."

"I won't be questioning him today. I will be observing and listening. I need to see how far Khora's roots are dug into his soul."

"I am still going."

"Rylan?"

"Aye ma'am. You are my family as much as he, and when he asks me to watch out for you, I'll guard you with my life."

"Boys," she shook her head and put her sunglasses on as they finally made their exit.

Linking her arm through his, they began their jaunt away from The Faerie Law Enforcement Consortium building.

The sun had warmed the air to a deliciously perfect temperature and Teagan relished the three blocks they had to walk to La Rose Gallery; the weather and the company helped her forget her impractical shoes. Olive Glasston, one of Teagan's oldest friends, shared curator and docent duties with Jonna; both provided some of the art for the studio as well. They were very talented and had become great friends since being chosen to run the business. Teagan had been trying for years to get Olive and Galen to date though both had resisted for one reason or another; she was sure they were perfect for each other and would not stop until one of them cried uncle.

La Rose Gallery was located in a strip mall in downtown Tucson. Set on the corner of one of the oldest streets in town, it took up nearly an entire block; the store front was whitewashed brick, large glass windows and double doors painted a shiny vermillion. The staff did not necessarily have a uniform but, the general standard was all black and business casual; brooding and hipster glasses were optional. Olive Glasston had perfected her work look over many years and today she looked every inch the knowledgeable curator; her rust-colored hair was pulled into a loose bun on the top of her head, the sleeves of her fitted black maxi dress came just to the elbow and she wore a length of perfectly polished Jade stones around her neck for a pop of color. There were a few customers being guided about by Teagan's sister-in-law Jonna, who had chosen a sleeveless black maxi dress and free flowing straight hair for the day; she had utilized her requisite violet framed eyeglasses as her own pop of color.

Galen and Teagan nodded at Jonna in greeting so as not to interrupt her work and made straight for Olive where she sat drawing at one of the large adjustable easels. The smell of crisp paper, canvas and acrylic paints were familiar and comforting; the perfectly polished white cement floor and soft lighting made one feel as though they were on a climate-controlled beach just before sunset. This was one of The Patrick family's favorite places to gather and Teagan always felt at home here.

"Hello love," Teagan greeted her friend brightly, removing her sunglasses as she did so.

"Ah my Scarlet Sister, how are you," Olive turned her swivel chair around to face her visitors.

"I am starving and taking you to lunch," Teagan informed her.

"I see," Olive chortled, "and you brought eye candy for my appetizer."

"Galen forced me to bring him along."

"Hello Olive, how are you?" Galen inclined his head toward her, his arms crossed behind his back.

"Much better now thanks," she winked back at him.

"Shall I leave you two alone then or, are you going to give me a hug and grab your things so we can be on our way?"

"I'll just be a moment," she rolled her eyes and rose to embrace Teagan.

The latter squeezed the former tightly, holding her as long as she would allow.

"Olive June Glasston! Since when do you wear men's cologne?"

"What?"

"You heard me. Either you have taken to wearing Galen's brand or, you didn't have a chance to shower after you spent the night at his house," Teagan poked Olive's ribs; grinning so widely her molars were visible.

"I don't know what you are speaking about," Olive shrugged her off and went to gather her purse from the employee's break room, leaving Teagan to turn on Galen and grill him instead.

"Listen here Murphy you can either tell me or, I'll procure it myself," crossing her arms over her chest and raising an eyebrow threateningly.

"I don't know what you are speaking of," he mimicked Olive's response; knowing that Teagan would never really read his mind in any instance less than dire.

"Either you tell me here or, I'll ask you in front of Jack and we both know he will take the mickey out of you if I do," she tapped her foot impatiently.

"Ugh, fine. We have gone out a few times, last night we had a bit too much to drink and she stayed over."

"Yeah she did," Teagan winked, grinning broadly again, her hands now on her hips.

"I slept on the couch Tea, nothing happened," he rolled his eyes at her but, could not keep his cheeks from flushing.

"Really nothing or, kind of nothing," Teagan teased.

"Gods, how far back is that break room," he feebly attempted to avoid answering.

"Uh huh, that's what I thought," Teagan giggled at his discomfort.

"Mostly nothing happened," he said suddenly interested in the shine on his shoes.

"Len, I have known Olive as long as you have known Rylan, there is no move that lady has that I don't know about, Drunken Damsel is old hat and the male is usually the only one drunk for it," Teagan informed the uncharacteristically surprised Galen.

"Here we go," Olive reappeared just in time to save Galen from further interrogation.

"Drunken Damsel, really?"

"What? He was nervous," Olive responded, putting her sunglasses on as they left the air-conditioned Gallery for natural air.

"Is he a good kisser?"

"I'm right here!"

"We know," the red-haired ladies said in unison to their

male counterpart trailing behind them as they exited the gallery and headed first south, then east to Jack's Bistro.

"Yes," Olive winked at Teagan.

"Gentlemen-zero, Olive-," Teagan started while she put her sunglasses back on.

"Let's not say exactly how successful that play is, there are some things better left a mystery," Olive interrupted hastily; eyes hidden by the dark lenses of her own aviator's.

"Thank you," Galen had matched their stride; looking sideways at Teagan, he took Olive's hand in his and kissed her palm.

"Gross," Teagan faked a grimace, "you don't know where her hands have been."

"Actually, I do," Galen winked at her, having finally regained his sense of humor.

"I might actually throw up," Teagan feigned nausea, which almost turned into real emesis due to her pregnant sensitivities. She paused a moment to steady her stomach, inciting a concerned look from her friends.

"I thought you were starving Madam, are we going too fast for you," Olive inquired seriously.

"No, no not too fast, I just faked vomit a little too well," Teagan lied; hopefully convincingly.

"Okay," Olive said suspiciously, narrowing her gaze at Teagan over her glasses before starting their journey again, though this time at a noticeably slower pace.

"Really doll, I'm alright," she took Olive's free hand reassuringly.

"Maybe you order the soup when we get to lunch," Olive suggested.

"Alright," Teagan smiled at her in answer.

They arrived at The Bistro after taking ten minutes longer than usual getting there at Olive's insistence that they take it easy. Bree was busy cleaning the glass front door with a rag when they rounded the corner; whistling a familiar tune and smiling as she worked.

"Hey lady," Teagan called as they approached.

"Hey friends," Bree responded brightly as she and Teagan hugged hello.

"I didn't know you were here today, I thought you'd be at The Pub."

"I am running all over the place this week," Bree smiled through her fatigue as she opened the door to let them through, "we are getting both businesses ready for your favorite holiday."

"St Paddy's Day," Olive said wistfully, "Good times, good times."

"Aye, it's always that sure," Galen nodded agreement.

"Speaking of fun and festivities Teagan, your mother has ordered at least two of everything off both menus," Bree shook her head; leading them to their usual table.

"Oh, that woman," Teagan said, rolling her eyes and tucking her sunglasses into her shirt pocket now that they were settled indoors again.

"Hello love," Jack had taken leave of his kitchen and sat down a moment to chat with his friends; he scooted in next to Teagan and kissed her cheek.

"Hey doll," she smiled back at him.

"Anything different than the usual," he asked.

"What is your soup today," Olive asked before Teagan could order her favorite lunch items.

"We have wild mushroom and quinoa or, parsnip and carrot."

"No. Move," Teagan insisted and pushed him out of the booth before she emptied what was left undigested from her breakfast into his lap. Nearly running down the hall to the bathroom, she got sick in a trash can by the kitchen before she could make it.

"Teagan are you okay," Olive's voice came over her shoulder.

"Can I get a washcloth or, something please," Teagan breathed deeply to steady her stomach.

"Sure," she went around her into the kitchen.

"Teagan if you're sick you should take the rest of the day off to rest; work will be there tomorrow," Bree rubbed her back in an attempt to comfort her.

"I'm not sick. I'll be fine. Can I get some mint or, something my mouth feels dirty," she requested, walking gingerly back to their table.

"Yes," Bree complied, passing Olive on her way back to the kitchen.

"Here you are doll," Olive handed her the cool washcloth she had asked for as they headed back to their table, "Teagan you can take a personal day you know."

"I am not sick," she mumbled from under the washcloth as Bree was returning with fresh mint leaves in hand, "I'm pregnant."

"What," her friends, save Galen, exclaimed at once.

"Why didn't you say anything," Bree admonished her.

"How far along are you," Olive couldn't contain her excitement.

"No wonder Lady Patrick ordered our whole menu twice over," Jack gave a characteristically ornery response.

"One at a time guys and Jack can I please get the mushroom soup with a large iced sweet tea."

"You've never had sweet tea a day in your life," finally the proprietor of their favorite bistro was surprised, "you must be pregnant."

"Jack, I'll have the usual," Galen placed his order while Jack was taking them down.

"No you won't, the smell of onions make me sick," pulling the wash cloth off her face; Teagan protested Galen's favorite onion rings on his turkey sandwich.

"Fine, the usual sans onion rings," he complied, "can I have jalapenos instead?"

"Yes," Teagan and Jack allowed simultaneously.

"I'll have the usual," Olive asked when she had finished giggling.

"Very well turkey burger, side of sweet potato fries and raspberry kombucha; everything with onions," Jack winked at Teagan.

"You best not bring anything with onions Jack Anthony unless you want to clean my sick off your shirt and send me home to an irate Mister McCarthy," Teagan glared at him.

"I'll get it started and be back to hear all about the magic of sprite growing," he waved off her threat and turned on his heel to get their meal together; firing up the oven first for the never actually ordered but always delivered anyway brussel sprout chips.

"I notice you've been quiet this whole time," Olive turned on Galen.

"Rylan told me two days ago," he shrugged, "he's terrible at keeping secrets."

"Is he now? And why didn't you tell me," Olive needled him.

"It wasn't mine to tell," Galen smiled.

"It still isn't," Teagan reminded him, "please don't say anything until we tell everyone."

"Fair enough and when will that be," Bree asked.

"We go to the doctor at the end of the week so, we'll tell everyone at the St Paddy's day party," she said taking a small sip from the large glass of tea Jack had just placed in front of her.

"I missed the part about your vagina right," he wrinkled his nose in faux disgust; sitting on the edge of the booth so he could grab their meals when they were ready.

"No we are just getting to it," Teagan teased.

"Well look at that saved by the bell," he jumped up from his seat when the bell on the front door jingled as a group of high school students entered the restaurant; Rylan McCarthy not far behind them.

"To what do I owe this pleasure darling," Teagan made to stand up when she saw him enter, white suspenders the only exception to his all-grey attire.

"You sit down young lady, I heard you were spilling your guts into a trash can," he sat down next to her, tucking a loose strand of hair behind her ear and kissing her forehead.

She breathed in his familiar musk and sighed deeply, snapping one of his suspenders against his chest playfully.

"Len, did you seriously call my husband?"

"No, I did," Bree said standing to clean an adjacent table, "I was worried and if you did need to go home you wouldn't have listened to anyone but Ry anyways."

"Thank you, friend," Rylan nodded at Breelan.

"I'm not a sprite you know, I can take care of myself," Teagan protested.

"A fine job you do of it, lass," Rylan assuaged his wife, "it's my job to take care of you too though and you aren't winning this one so, let it be."

"Aye sir," she pouted.

"Pouting are we," Rylan laughed down at her, "I thought you weren't a sprite?"

"I'm not," she frowned, "but, I don't have to be happy about the cavalry being called in unnecessarily."

"It was necessary love. I'll go as soon as I see you've had some food in you, and you've kept it down."

"Good job knocking up your hot wife by the way," Olive winked at Rylan.

"And I thought I was the one who couldn't keep a secret Galen?"

"Don't look at me McCarthy, it was your hot wife."

"You knew they were dating," Teagan huffed at her husband.

"Of course I did, he can't keep anything from me," he took a long drink from Teagan's glass of sweet tea.

"You two are worse than girls," she rolled her eyes at them.

"I can't believe you ordered this," Rylan smacked his lips, "if I was unsure you were pregnant before, I'm not now. What else did you order? I'm starving."

"Mushroom soup," Jack announced, placing a large steaming bowl in front of her after their chips had been set down in the middle of the table.

"That smells fantastic, I'll have the same and a sweet tea as well please," Rylan asked.

"You got it. Did you want salad today too? Quinoa and kale," Jack offered.

"Yes, and for Teagan too, please," Rylan requested.

"No," she protested, "that's too much food and I'll be quinoaed out by the end of it."

"You need to eat please love and if you don't finish, you can always take it with you for later; I'm sure you'll be hungry again in about two hours anyway."

"I'm not sure I like this telling me what to do business," she frowned, dipping her spoon into her bowl for a bite.

"I'm not sure why you're surprised," Rylan responded around a mouthful of ice, "I've been telling you what to do for years."

"Rylan Robert, you bite your tongue! I have a reputation to uphold," she joked.

"Good luck with that, you're pregnant now the jig is up," he rolled his eyes.

"Here you are dear," back from the kitchen, Bree gently placed Rylan's food in front of him and sat down on the other side of Teagan, "Jack should be just behind me with the rest."

"Now, where were we," Jack chimed in before setting down the rest of everyone's order and taking his own seat next to Olive.

"Yes Ollie, where were we," Teagan raised a brow.

"Baby names I think" she grinned into her burger.

"Negative. How long have you two been secretly dating?"

"Two months," Galen answered before taking a large bite of his sandwich.

"Two months," Teagan swallowed hard to avoid choking on her quinoa.

"Come on now mama red, don't be mad," Rylan rubbed her back, "they just wanted to be sure it would stick before telling everyone. Surely you can understand that."

"You would've been the first person I told lady," Olive assured Teagan, "trust."

"I'll keep that in mind when sending out baby shower invitations," Teagan grinned mischievously.

"Seriously? Do not be upset about this," Olive rolled her eyes.

"I'm just pouting. You know I like to know everything."

"We know," the table of Folk said in unison, to a somewhat miffed Teagan; before their second fit of laughter that afternoon.

Curious

After dropping what was left of their lunch at the office, they strolled arm in arm admiring the creatures in their exhibits before turning their attention to surveying the Queen lunching in the park. Teagan's favorite part of any zoo was always the Polar Bear and Elephant habitats, and Galen indulged her feeding the Giraffes as well before buying her popcorn to feed the ducks. It never ceased to amaze Teagan how little human beings paid attention; gathered around the west edge of the duck pond were no less than twenty Faeries. The woman at the center of their group was sitting ankles crossed on a sumptuous looking emerald-green silk cushion, her face hidden by the black veil that matched the cotton dress covering her from head to toe. It could be anyone under that fabric but if rumors could be believed, which Teagan seldom did, it was Queen Khora; her thoughts and energy did not contradict said rumors. Presently she was entertaining herself by feeding the ducks, reaching a black leather gloved hand into the red and white striped paper sack full of popcorn every few minutes to dust the surface of the lake. She was alternately sipping tea and taking small bites from a large, overly marzipanned cake when she wasn't providing the too fat fowl with their salty snack. She had four elf guards stationed at various posts around her party.

Naturally the one Teagan was after stood closest to The Queen; Orion Red Birch was as handsome as the star he was named for, hair black and shiny as crow feathers fell in a neat braid to the middle of his back, his deep orange eyes scanned the landscape before him meticulously and his lean body gracefully bore the heavy silver armor his station required. His chain mail gloved right hand rested lightly on the haft of the broadsword sheathed at his waist and he shifted only slightly when he spotted Teagan strolling in his vicinity. He looked right through her and like any good soldier, gave no indication that anything was out of sorts.

Teagan did not spot the Feandragoon until it was almost on her shoulder. It was all she could do to contain a schoolgirl squeal; there was nothing could be done about the glee that flushed her cheeks. It was a beautiful creature and the only one of its kind that Teagan had ever seen. Teagan believed, as many did, that they were an old elven myth. Feandragoons are miniature versions of Dragons though they are far more powerful than their full-sized cousins and care not for gold or, treasure. Their sole purpose is to act as guardians of Elves who are pure of heart. Once an elf was claimed by a Feandragoon, they were bonded for life; one was never without the other. This particular Dragoon was slightly smaller than most, if the tales were to be believed and elves were trustworthy more often than not. It was about eight inches form snout to tail and its wingspan was just over twelve inches. The tough hide resembled that of a June bug, shiny black save for when the sunlight hit at just the right angle, then it was a vision of greens, blues and purples. The slightly softer underbelly was a pale ivory, though Teagan was sure no one would ever get close enough to test just how soft it actually was.

The little dragon landed softly on her left shoulder as she and Galen meandered along the path around the lake; stopping only to shower the surface with popcorn for the ducks. The Dragoon had pushed through her blocks and Teagan heard a sweet female voice trickle through her mind.

'Good afternoon, Teagan the Mute. My companion wishes to speak with you but, for now will only do so through me. My name is Airioch and I am pleased to make your acquaintance.'

She had the voice of a British youth and pronounced her name Air-e-yah. It was the Gaelic word for caretaker, Teagan felt it quite fitting.

'Teagan the Mute,' she chucked audibly, *'I've not been called that for a very long time. Hello Airioch, it's lovely to meet you. To be clear, the companion you're speaking for is Orion?'*

'Aye. Orion Red Birch is my charge and I his guardian.'

'Very well. Tell him I will speak through you for now.'

'Good. Orion Red Birch sends this warning; "Do not seek what you are not prepared to find."'

'Meaning?'

'The answers you want are complex. If you kick over a rock in the desert, know that scorpions lie beneath.'

'How many?'

'Enough.'

'Poisonous?'

'Are there another kind?'

'Lethal?'

'Yes.'

Teagan pondered this warning for a moment as they rounded the eastern edge of the water and began to head north. She splashed the cool water with the last of their popcorn and handed Galen the grease-soaked empty sack to dispose of as he made for the exit to wait for her.

'Tell Orion Red Birch that Teagan the Mute will meet him tonight. Mother Hubbard's. 6 pm.'

The response came only moments later.

'He'll be there.'

Airioch pushed off so gently Teagan did not know she was gone until she flew across her field of vision back to her companion. Teagan had to force herself to walk normally as she left so as not to raise any suspicion, from the Fae party at the lake or, from her coworker.

"Well," Galen inquired anxiously, matching her pace and the seriousness in her tone.

"I've set a meeting with him for tonight. Mother Hubbard's. 1800."

"Good. We can set up at the bike shop nearby."

"Right. Let's get ready."

Teagan sat at her favorite booth in one of her favorite restaurants in town, tapping her fingers anxiously on the cup of decaf English breakfast steeping itself on the table in front of her.

"Something's wrong," she said aloud. To anyone eavesdropping she appeared to have said it to herself but, Galen and a few of his squad had chosen the booth behind her for surveillance; just in case the interrogation went south.

"Hey bro, what time you got," Galen's faux frat boy voice issued loudly in acknowledgement from his post behind her.

"It's only five minutes to 6 dude, We have plenty of time," Officer Walsh responded in a less believable 'bro' voice.

"He won't show," Teagan admonished them both but, directed the statement at her teacup. Orion was many things but, late and inaccessible weren't among his traits.

Teagan and Orion had been high school sweethearts though, graduation was where their romantic relationship ended. Orion was very much in love with her and prepared to settle down as soon as she gave the word. His only apprehension was that she refused to let him in. She had never been a great communicator but, as a sprite she was awful; poor Orion had to practically pull teeth to get minimal amounts of information out of her. Especially if that information was how she felt about something. She was not good with feelings; she saw them as nasty, inconvenient things that got in the way of logic. She loved Orion immensely but, she could never articulate it properly.

She was certain he would never fully understand her and did not want to inflict her insecurities upon him; she was still supremely uncomfortable with her uniqueness in her formative years. When she did finally tell him how she felt it was too late and was not nearly enough to make up for the grief she had given him. Patience was definitely one of his many virtues; he should probably have been sainted after the ass pain that was his relationship with Teagan Patrick. Their parents, having known each other since her father was a sprite himself, were disappointed there would not be a blending of the Patrick and Red Birch families. Everyone had remained close friends, however and may as well have been family; they were certainly in each other's business enough to be considered as much.

"You being stood up hon? I'm sure that hubby of yours has got caught up at school and just lost track of time," Tom the middle-aged waiter reassured her; smiling broadly with the few teeth he had left. He carefully set her order of waffles and potatoes in front of her, winking before he made his way back to the kitchen. She poured cinnamon agave over the blue corn waffles she regularly craved and cut into her first bite. Her nerves getting the better of her, she swallowed hard to prevent it coming right back up and washed it down with a mouthful of tea.

"Oi! Tommy! Can we get the check please," Galen called to the kitchen suddenly.

"So lame that your girl can't let you have brinner with us," Officer Walsh teased Officer Cole; indicating to Teagan that something indeed had gone wrong and they'd been called out.

"Yeah man, what can I say? Your boy does work and when she calls I've got to go to it," Cole feigned arrogantly back in his SoCal diction.

Just then Teagan's cell phone buzzed indicating she had a message.

'We got a call out. Code Eleven,' Galen's text message read.

'Murder? Color me surprised. 10-4,' Teagan sent back.

Well, Teagan thought to herself, hopefully I'll be able to finish my own "brinner" before I'm called in. I'd hate to leave these house potatoes unfinished. The TAC Squad paid for their meals and left hurriedly. She received her own call with one forkful left on her plate, placed a twenty-dollar bill on the table and nodded goodbye to the kitchen staff.

She sent Rylan a text message while she walked to the park letting him know she would be home a bit late and not to wait up for her, then placed her phone on silent mode.

When she arrived on scene, it had long been secured by patrol before Galen and the TAC Squad had arrived to take over. She found Orion sprawled face down in his own blood on the sidewalk near the west side of the duck pond she had strolled earlier; his amber eyes wide open and unseeing, his mouth agape in a silent scream. Teagan knelt down at his right side and gingerly moved his long dark hair away from his face with the end of her pen. A large angry purple bruise had blossomed just above his collar bone where his neck and shoulder met. Two slightly darker, circle shaped marks were barely visible in the center of the bruise; suggesting his blood had been drained. By an actual Vampire or, made to look like one had drained him Teagan could not decipher from the confused and inconsistent energy saturating the atmosphere.

She could feel the blonde Reaver from the previous night had been here but, as companion or assailant was unclear. Whoever actually killed Orion had hastily covered their tracks with literally, stolen energy. This was frightening and infuriating. Her coworkers had impatiently and with bated breath held their positions around the crime scene while she worked. Overcome with anxiety and disgust at the scene before her, she stood up too quickly and nearly tripped in her haste to get to the nearest trash can. A few dry heaves later and she was emptying her barely digested waffles into the bottom of the bin.

"Contact Trinity Red Birch and have her meet me at the station in an hour. She will already know why but, under no circumstances are you to give her details. She will pry so keep your thoughts on anything else other than what you have seen this night, and don't take any refreshment she offers or your other precautions will be for nothing," she instructed Detective Smith.

"Yes ma'am," he responded quietly.

He was scared and seriously reconsidering his assignment to the unit. The senior Detective felt bad for the rookie but, this was not a job for just anyone and if he knew now that he couldn't handle it, he should admit as much and save everyone the headache.

"Galen did you see the Feandragoon when you arrived?"

"No. No one was here except the Parks and Rec guy. He was the one who found the body," he replied handing her a sanitizing wipe for her face and hands as well as sterile gloves so she could start poking about the crime scene without leaving her fingerprints behind.

"He's already being transported to the station?"

"Yes. Sergeant Thaumes took him just before you arrived."

"Good. Have Crime Scene do their full work up. I want their report on my desk first thing tomorrow."

"You got it," Galen nodded.

"And Galen, search the entire park. I want to know exactly which scorpions we freed from the rocks earlier."

"Yes ma'am," he understood she suspected The UnSeelie Queen was responsible.

Lady Trinity Red Birch was waiting in her office when she arrived a little less than an hour later. Whatever she had been interrupted doing, grief did nothing to diminish her ethereal beauty. Her long black hair was brushed into a loose chignon at the nape of her neck. The dark green caftan suited her perfectly toned willowy self impeccably as did the knee high dark brown leather boots; any photographer worth his salt would drool over how flawless her skin was sans makeup.

She stood when Teagan opened the door, and they embraced each other gently.

"Lady Trinity," Teagan bowed respectfully to her mentor after they let go their hug.

"Princess," the elf inclined her head in kind.

"Ugh not tonight I'm not. They don't let me wear my tiara to the office," she attempted to lighten the mood as she rolled her eyes and took her seat.

Trinity smiled sadly as she took the well cushioned seat of her own across from Teagan's desk. The latter breathed deeply and looked straight in the former's eyes.

"Lady Trinity Red Birch it is my deepest regret and with sincere apology I must inform you that your son, Orion Red Birch, was murdered this night. I cannot express to you how truly sorry I am for your loss."

"I know. Thank you for telling me yourself, My little Teagan the Mute."

"That's the second time in a hundred years I've been called that, and both were by Red Birches on the same day. That's how I knew he was in trouble."

"You know, I was always disappointed that you two couldn't make it work," the elf lamented with furrowed brow.

"I know but, you know all too well that we are too much alike. *Were*. We *were* too much alike. I cannot believe he is gone," the faerie rubbed her forehead hard and shook a tear from her lashes.

"Me neither. I feared this would be his fate though."

"You knew he was in the employ of the Unseelie Queen then?"

"Of course. He took the post against his better judgment and many warnings on my part."

"Why did he take it then?"

"Truthfully?"

"Please."

"Your father planted him as a spy."

"What for?"

"There have been too many dead Folk of late. He believed the Queen was behind it but, needed proof."

"I thought the King was behind it? I know The UnSeelie Royals are estranged but..."

"My darling," Trinity cut her off, "there has not been a Winter King for almost two hundred years."

"What?"

"He disappeared before Tylane did. It's more likely that Khora killed him in a rage than for him to have run off with a consort."

"Why isn't this common knowledge?"

"If you were the head of The Winter Court, you wouldn't want your enemies to know how few your numbers were, how weak you were, would you?"

"No, no I would not," Teagan responded, her mind spinning with all the new information, "So, Tylane is probably dead. The Winter King is most likely also dead, and The Winter Queen is what...killing Folk for sport?"

"So it would seem."

"It doesn't make sense. Why draw attention to oneself

unnecessarily? Grief stricken or, not. Mad or, not; she's smarter than that," the detective thought aloud.

"Is she? Or, is she trying to incite another war so she can finish what her daughter started?"

"I would lay low personally but, you do make a good point. 'There's no hate as deep as the hate that springs in Winter,'" Teagan recited an old adage about The UnSeelie Court.

"Indeed."

"Do you want to head over to the house? I've got some work to finish but, Rylan is never too busy for a drink," Teagan suggested, smiling politely.

"Oh, I think I'll just head home dear."

"Are you sure? I don't want you to be alone Lady. Perhaps a whiskey with Father?"

"No Child. Thank you but, I want to be alone just now. Sort out my thoughts," she shrugged weakly.

"Alright then. If you need anything I'll be listening," she winked and tapped her temple.

"I know," Trinity smiled at her, "I love you Princess."

"I love you back Lady. Oh, and Trinity?"

"Yes dear?"

"You're sure you can't think of anyone save The Queen who would do this to Orion? Augustana maybe?"

"Augustana Von Dotch? No. They were engaged to be married. He asked only yesterday. Not my first choice but, they loved each other deeply."

"I see," Teagan paused for a breath and to think before she spoke again, "I only ask because The Banshee never arrived."

"Didn't she? Well, that *is* interesting," for the first time since she'd known her, Trinity looked frightened and was avoiding Teagan's gaze.

"Is it possible that she was working for The Queen?"

"I suppose anything is possible," Trinity's disbelief barely audible.

"You never tried to read her?"

"She was dating my son," raised eyebrow and judgmental smirk were confirmation enough for the detective.

"And?"

"And she was a murderer but, as noble a murderer as I've ever met," Trinity shook her head and wrung her hands in an uncharacteristic gesture of anxiety.

"You're sure?"

"Yes Teagan, I'm sure," Trinity nodded fervently.

"She is a Reaver though, maybe she gave in to her carnal nature?"

"I do not believe she would but again, anything is possible."

"Fair enough then," Teagan stood indicating their interview was over for now and met Trinity at the door.

"See you Friday."

"Aye," she said into Trinity's shoulder as they hugged before parting ways; she offered to walk her home but, was again politely refused by the elf before she went on her way.

Teagan closed the door and locked it after her mentor left. Collapsing in her chair under the weight of the day's events she breathed deeply and checked her phone for the first time in hours. There was a text message from Rylan.

'There is a Feandragoon waiting in the kitchen for you, my love. Come home soon.'

Three hours later than she usually worked while on a day

shift, Teagan was greeted in her kitchen by a shirtless and sweaty Rylan and an anxious Airioch; *'When the Levee Breaks'* playing in the background when she arrived was apropos and she chuckled at the irony as she closed and locked their back door.

"It's a good thing I was working out back or, she'd have been on the stoop a long time," Rylan crunched around a hunk of ice from his half full water glass.

'Hello again Detective. Or, is it Princess?'

'Neither. Please, call me Teagan.'

"She'd have let you know she was here love," she said into his salty neck when she hugged him, pushing out of her heels with her toes and kicking them off when she settled back down to the floor from their embrace.

"You smell good," his deep voice rumbled through her hair.

"So do you. What have you been at that's got you so sweaty," she asked pulling back to look at his face.

"Come here, I'll show you," he grinned boyishly at her, set down his glass and took her hand to lead her down the hall. She was all too happy to delay speaking about Orion.

'May I come too?'

'Yes Airioch, climb on,' Teagan offered her shoulder.

The door was ajar when they arrived in front of the room set just off the kitchen; the baby's room smelled like anise and cedar. Rylan had already engraved a protection rune into the solid cherry wood. Teagan ran her thumb over it when he pulled her over the threshold after him.

"Close your eyes now," he said before turning on the light, "no peeking."

"Aye sir," she replied through her smile. She heard the switch flip up and Airioch's voice whisper across her mind.

'Oh Teagan, its lovely'

"Open your eyes love," Rylan's stubble dusted chin scratched against her forehead.

She did as she was told, and tears immediately burned at the back of her eyes.

While she was stuck at work, Rylan cut, stained and hammered together their child's crib. She left him standing in the doorway and walked over to admire his handiwork more closely.

"Don't touch it yet, it's still drying," he warned, rushing to pull her hand back from the wet, onyx-stained cedar creation taking up the center of the otherwise empty room.

"You're amazing," she whispered before kissing the back of his right hand.

'It smells comfortable in here.'

'Doesn't it? Do you think a baby will like it,' she asked Airioch as she strolled around the large room, running the hand that wasn't cradling her belly along the teal walls. Teal had not been Rylan's first choice of room color but, was an acceptable compromise after too many hours spent discussing it. They had painted it together the weekend before last and Olive would be painting a mural on the west wall the weekend after next. She refused to tell them exactly what she had planned. She wanted to surprise them so all they knew was that it would include a ship and possibly sea creatures.

'Oh yes, he will love it! Do you have a name?'

"Rylan, what are we going to call him?"

"Are we entirely sure we are having a 'he," he asked hugging her from behind.

"Yes," she said aloud as Airioch echoed it in her head, both laughed simultaneously at their jinxing one another.

"I'm assuming the giggle fit is because the Dragoon agrees with you," Rylan laughed at them, "what does she sound like?"

"Like a proper British Lady. She is very sweet."

'British Lady? Thank you, Irish Pixie.'

'You're welcome.'

"Ah I see. Will our Duchess Airioch be staying with us long?"

"Good question, hang on."

'Airioch are you able to stay here? Neither of us is pure of heart or, any other vital organ to be sure.'

'No,' she said chuckling, 'but, there is one of this house who is pure of heart.'

"She can stay because of our son!"

"Brilliant! Let's figure a name for our little chap then, shall we?"

"Hmm...what about Bryan?"

'Boru is the only Brian I've ever known...He had a dreadful temper,' Airioch snorted disapproval.

"After my father? No thank you."

"Alright then, Airioch agrees anyway. What about Ethan?"

"Ethan? Are swirly's fashionable again? I didn't know."

"Wow," she rolled her eyes at him, "what about William?"

'Oh, William is lovely and very noble.'

"We have too many Williams in our family tree."

"Alright, Prince Rylan the Persnickety, what have you come up with then?"

'I knew a Prince once who was known as The Persnickety. Rylan isn't nearly so bad, and he is certainly much more handsome.'

'Is that right? Thank you. I'll let him know, shall I?'

'Goodness no!'

'Is that a blush milady,' Teagan teased Airioch.

'Oh stop!'

"How about Liam," he suggested after thinking a moment.

"Liam but, not William? Nay."

"Hmm...how about Jameson?"

"As what? An homage to how he got here? No sir."

"Fine then, named for whiskey he won't be. Maybe Peter?"

"Do we want him hanging about with unpredictable blonde pixies and making off with children in the night? Please tell me you aren't serious," she scoffed.

'That is a tale that has been greatly exaggerated,' Airioch mirrored Teagan's scoff.

"I'm beginning to see why people get divorced after children," he teased her.

"Because the men who father them have terrible taste in names? I agree with your assessment entirely," she teased back.

"Okay let's get serious," he tugged her hair so that her face turned up at him.

"I was being serious!"

"I get the crib in the divorce then."

"What?! And leave your child homeless in addition to nameless? I think I've chosen my baby daddy poorly," she winked up at him.

"Clearly our child is doomed to terrible parents," he kissed her forehead before releasing his hold on her hair.

"Ever the stubborn faeries are we," she chuckled.

"I am the Rhett to your Scarlett darling."

'Oh! You're not nearly spoiled enough to be Scarlett!'

'My husband would certainly argue that dear but, thank you.'

"What about Rhett?"

"Ever?"

"Everette?"

"Everette. I love it."

"Everette Rylan," she said now turned toward him and standing on tip toes to meet his gaze, "your name should be his middle name."

"Everette Rylan" he rested his forehead on hers.

"Everette Rylan," she said softly into his mouth before kissing him.

"I'm glad that's settled then. What kept you late at work wife?"

"Orion Red Birch is dead," she let her heels fall back to the floor and looked down at their toes to avoid his curious baby blues.

"I figured that's how we ended up with Airioch. What happened?"

"He was murdered."

'He was murdered,' Airioch's melancholy matched Teagan's.

"Are you okay?"

"I think so."

"Why won't you look at me?"

"I will be better when we find his killer," she said looking up at him.

'Airioch do you know who murdered Orion?'

"Did Airioch see who killed him," Rylan asked Teagan just as she asked the same of the little dragon.

'Oh, Teagan I wish I could help. One moment we were walking around the lake with Augustana, the next Orion was on the ground bleeding and she was screaming for help.'

"She says no," Teagan frowned.

'You're sure it wasn't Augustana?'

'It definitely wasn't. It couldn't have been or, I'd have killed her.'

"Are there any creatures that can mute her kind of magic?"

'No.'

"No. Is there any magic you can mute or repel Airioch?"

'The only beings that cannot see me are those who are truly self-ish; my magic repels those who would manipulate or misuse me.'

"The Queen?"

'It is possible. I have never seen her.'

'Because she is repelled by you?'

'No because she is covered from head to foot with the hideous black frocks she wears.'

'She cannot see you though?'

'Correct.'

"Ahem, some of us don't hear everyone's thoughts," Rylan gave a familiar reminder.

"Right, sorry. She says she wouldn't recognize The Queen but, The Queen doesn't know about her so Airioch isn't in any danger. Andreaus may well be involved in this."

"Dominus?!"

'I didn't even think of him! Stealth is the way he operates, I wouldn't have seen him.'

"Is there another?"

"That man is everywhere! We heard stories about him when we were sprites," Rylan failed keeping his inner fan boy at bay.

"Why are you boys so delighted at the mere mention of his name? My brothers always idolized him too," Teagan huffed.

"He is just so bad ass. Here in a flash, handling business, probably boffed your mother and gone just as quick," Rylan grinned dreamily, "bad ass."

"Whatever," Teagan rolled her eyes.

"Don't 'whatever' me young lady," Rylan feigned chastising his wife.

"Whatever," she stuck her tongue out at him.

"Oh, very mature Princess," he said to her back as she left their child's room with their newly acquired Feandragoon.

"I'll show you mature," she winked at him over her shoulder.

"Teagan McCarthy! Not in front of the dragoon!"

'It's time for me to hunt anyway.'

'Be safe and knock before you come back.'

'I'll do that,' she chuckled and flew toward the front door, materializing through the other side effortlessly.

"Cool," the McCarthy's exclaimed simultaneously.

"Now, about that maturity you planned on showing me," Rylan took Teagan by the hand and led her back to their room, making sure to close the door lest Airioch see more of them than any of them wished her to.

Distress

The day had finally come for what would be the first of many check-ups during Teagan's pregnancy. After a lengthy argument they left an indignant Airioch at home, The Mc-Carthy's arrived early for their appointment and were glad they did. It was very busy, and Doctor Monaghan was eager to get to her last appointment of the day. The nurse, Aerine, had school bus yellow skin and entirely black eyes that contrasted her pastel purple hair, though to any humans attending hospital she looked an average middle-aged nurse. She led them from the waiting room toward the area in the back where exams rooms were kept and instructed Teagan to take off her boots and step on the scale; she took a deep breath and did as she was told.

"Alright little lady, you're a little over five feet six inches and about 135 pounds," announced the nurse as she wrote it in the chart, "Lucky duck, you'll probably be able to eat whatever you want for the next nine months!"

"Not much will have changed then," Rylan winked at his wife.

Stepping back and gathering her boots, Aerin led them to their exam room and a waiting Doctor Monaghan.

"Hello dears," she greeted them with a tired smile, "I'll leave a moment and let you shuck those jeans Teagan."

She and Aerin exited the room leaving a nervous couple behind them. Teagan stripped her jeans and underwear and put on the paper robe she was provided. In an uncharacteristic move, Rylan did not watch his wife during this process and merely looked half interested at the paintings lining the wall. She had just sat down on the exam table when Doctor Monaghan reentered the room with Aerin in her wake, both carrying several items including Teagan's chart.

"Alright ma'am, shall we get started," she asked setting down her cache and washing her hands. Putting on her exam gloves and preparing the speculum, she rolled over on her chair and asked Teagan to "lie back and scoot all the way to the end of the table." Rylan continued burning a hole in the floor with his gaze, cheeks nearly as red as his wife's hair.

"*What's wrong,*" Teagan pressed through their mental bond.

"*I've never had to deal with anyone else being that close to your vagina,*" he thought still looking at the floor. Stifling a laugh, Teagan stared at the ceiling as her exam commenced.

Satisfied that all was well with Teagan, Aerin prepared and handed the doctor the ultrasound transducer so they could check on the baby.

"This is going to be a little cold," Doctor Monaghan told Teagan as she squirted ice cold blue jelly on her stomach.

Spreading it around with the transducer as she looked for a heartbeat, Teagan held her breath and hoped for the best. Suddenly a sound like galloping horses filled the silent room and broke the tension that could be cut with a knife. Nearly jumping from his chair, Rylan took the few steps toward his wife and held her hand in both of his. Kissing her forehead as she tried to hold back her tears of joy, "That's our little man," he whispered. She could feel his smile against her skin and let loose a sigh of relief.

"That's him. That's really him," she grinned up at her husband and let all her emotions pour down her cheeks.

"Congratulations, you're definitely pregnant," Doctor Monaghan beamed at them, "You're about twelve weeks so, your due date will be around October 8th. We'll want to get you started on some vitamins right away and schedule your next appointment. Do you want to know the gender?"

"Yes," they exclaimed simultaneously.

"You are indeed having a boy," Doctor Monaghan revealed chuckling at them through her broad smile. Wiping the jelly off her stomach, Teagan was now free to put her pants back on and ask any questions she or, Rylan had of the doctor. As neither had any, they were given a list of instructions, prescriptions for prenatal vitamins and anti-nausea medications and were set on their way. Excited to finally share the happy news with everyone later that evening, they paid little attention as they chattered like monkeys while exiting the office and entering the main wing of the hospital. It would be the best offering they could bring to their Family's increasingly extravagant Saint Patrick's Day festivities.

Walking hand in hand toward the front of the building they basked in the joy of their good fortune and did not notice the corridor they had come from growing dark.

A few seconds later they heard screams and turned to see smoke coming from the offices behind them. Letting go his wife's hand and propelling her forward, 'run,' Rylan urged inside her head. Listening with her ears and probing with her mind as she ran, Teagan did not notice anything out of the ordinary. Screams and panic aside, it was business as usual; no one calmer than they should be or thinking ominous thoughts. There was a hole. Some one here was blocking her and she could not tell how or, who it was. She and Rylan kept running toward the exit as fast as they could but something was pulling against them. Teagan tried to gain control of their surroundings but, was rebuffed violently and nearly knocked over by the force. The smoke was growing thicker, the screams louder when a percussion grenade exploded only thirty feet behind them. Shielding her from the blast, Rylan turned after the noise had dissipated and saw a tall, imposing figure coming at them from the wall of smoke. Momentarily dumb struck by what was in front of him Rylan froze, the assailant took this window of opportunity to throw another grenade directly at them. With no time to avoid the blast Rylan shoved his wife as hard as he could away from him toward the open office door adjacent to them and made to follow her. Tumbling into the empty office, the last thing she saw was the look on Rylan's face, a mixture of panic, confusion and fear. She had only ever seen that look once before and it was she who had been the cause.

She heard the blast, something solid hit the ground with a sickening thud and an acrid stench filled her lungs. She was still aware of Rylan so, knew he was alive at least though in what state she could not be sure. She took a deep breath to steady her nerves and low crawled across the floor to the threshold of the room. Peeking around the corner in the direction of the fray, she could see two figures. Rylan was on the ground completely still aside from shallow breathing. The man standing over him was her brother-in-law, Blair Davies. Leaning down to check the body and appearing to check the pulse, "Damn," he growled angrily. He turned on his heel and went back in the direction of the destruction he had caused, limping slightly as he hastened away from Rylan's body. Teagan tried to get inside his head but, to no avail. Pushing so hard she made herself dizzy, she stopped before harming herself further and ruining any chance she had of saving Rylan. This was the strangest thing she had encountered since Wednesday night, and it did not ease the panic from her thoughts. As soon as he was gone, she crawled to her husband, checking to make sure he was still with her. He was indeed alive but, only just.

Picking him up she flew, literally, out of the building toward their home; calling out to her father as she went.

'Athair! Athair,' she pushed urgently into her father's mind.

'Teagan,' he responded almost instantly, *'what's wrong Rua?'*

'We've been attacked! Blair Davies bombed Bansail Hospital and Rylan's been injured...badly. Send the TAC Team there and send armed escort to meet us at home,' she instructed.

'Done,' was all the answer he gave, and all the answer Teagan needed.

Tears began to fall down her smoke smudged cheeks as panic threatened to take over her faculties. Breathing deeply and moving higher into the cool atmosphere, she ignored the chill setting into their clothes and began to think a happy memory to distract herself; May Day long ago when she and Rylan introduced their families for the first time.

Her mother loved entertaining and tonight was no

exception. Rose Hagan Patrick flitted about with extra fervor, her tiny frame nearly a blur as she prepared their home for two very important guests. Tonight, she was hosting her daughters' suitors. Matthew had officially asked to court Meagan weeks ago but, this was the first time she would meet Rylan. She had never seen Teagan so smitten and was interested to know the source. She loved her children and loved who they loved while they loved them at least. She had known Bryan McCarthy for years as one of her husband's childhood acquaintances and was not surprised their children had gotten along famously.

Putting the finishing touches on their formal dining room and giving her coddle one last stir she headed upstairs to get ready.

Nearly running into her husband as she opened their bedroom door, she gathered her senses as he pretended to scold her "Aye woman! Slow down before you hurt yourself!" He chuckled, picking her up in a tight bear hug.

"Hello, my love," she mumbled into his chest. Breathing him in deeply, her nervous energy was immediately calmed by his presence. He had always had this effect on her. He had that effect on most people actually; his gift was that of balance. He had the ability to control energy and emotion. His real talent lay in his musicianship though. That was where his passion lie and his wife loved to hear him sing more than she loved almost anything else in the world. Standing on her tip toes for a kiss, he leaned down to meet her lips with his before untangling themselves and going about dressing for the evening.

After changing into what his wife had lain out for him,

Timothy Patrick walked down the hallway to his daughters' room. They didn't need to share but, chose to do so out of fondness for each other and for fashion; they used Meagan's room as a closet. Adjusting his tie and straightening his back he knocked before entering.

"Hello Father," they said in unison; their voices, much like nearly every physical aspect, almost identical.

"Hello dears," he responded smiling warmly at their backs as they finished getting ready. Teagan, as usual, was finished first and turned to her father for approval. Mother had insisted they dress semi formally for dinner. It was a special occasion yes but, they were at home and she wished her children to be comfortable.

For Teagan this meant she wore a white cotton summer dress with a pale pink ribbon at the low-cut neckline, elbows and waist, her hair in a single plait that fell to the middle of her back and no makeup aside from mascara and blush.

"You look lovely my dear," he said brushing the back of her hand with a kiss, "Rylan will certainly be eating from the palm of your hand if he isn't already."

"Thank you Athair," she smiled at him as she left the room and her family chattering about their visitors.

Meagan was beside herself with nerves. She had never been courted and was so fond of Matthew that she didn't know what she'd do if he didn't like her family or, worse the other way around! Teagan laughed inwardly at the trifles of young love. She was in love with Rylan but, neither cared if their families liked the other. It didn't really matter to them as they were courting each other, not their families. She would be more concerned if her friends didn't like Rylan and for the first time began to wonder when they would meet. This tangent quickly leaped to another in which she began to get nervous at having a long-distance relationship. She lived in Douglas with her family and Rylan in Kinsale with his. Frowning at the thought of seeing each other less often than they do now, she suddenly found herself in the formal dining room where the maids were setting the table and walked straight through to the kitchen where her mother was finishing up dinner. Teagan was convinced that her mother was so lovely she could make a flour sack look fashionable. Tonight, she had chosen a soft cotton dress the color of crushed primrose with sleeves just past her elbows, the neckline hit just at her collar bone and fell straight to the floor. No ribbon to draw attention to her tiny waist.

She was adding a pinch of sea salt to her coddle and ladling it into one of the large stone serving crocks her grandmother had given her parents as a wedding gift. She practically jumped a mile when Teagan placed a hand between her shoulder blades, catching her off guard she was so engrossed with the meal she had spent all day preparing.

"Tea! You scared me half to death," she mock scolded her daughter. Handing the first of two soon to be full crocks of coddle to Lucy, one of the house maids, she gave her second youngest a tight hug and kissed her on the cheek.

"I'd have liked to hear you wail like a banshee," smiling widely at her mother's feigned scowl.

"I'm sure you would've einin! Rotten children, the lot of you."

"Ah we are that indeed but, you made us so."

"I blame your father."

"So do I. Speaking of father, I have a question."

"Ask."

Scooting onto the counter adjacent to the stove her mother was making good use of, Teagan sat crossed legged and began picking raisins off of a loaf of freshly baked bread.

"If he decides to give Rylan and I his permission to court, how would that work?" "How do you mean?"

"I mean Rylan is here and I am with you in Douglas. How would we have a relationship so far away from each other?"

"My goodness you're nervous! Stop taking it out on the bread will you," her mother chastised and moved the bread away from her anxious daughter.

Teagan only rolled her eyes and tucked her hands beneath her knees in response.

"It's a good thing you're Fae and can fly wherever you wish."

"I know but, that's an awfully long way isn't it?"

"Teagan Inez Patrick, you are falling in love with this boy. Don't you try to talk yourself out of it and don't try to get me to talk you out of it either."

"Rotten though we may be, you do know us all, that's certain."

"Aye, I do and don't you forget it either."

Lucy had returned just then and was standing by while her mother began to fill the last crock with piping hot food. Teagan's stomach grumbled audibly and she tried to cover it up by jumping down off the counter to resume their conversation.

"I just mean there is so much that could happen between now and when we go home and when we are home who's to say someone won't catch my eye? Who's to say Rylan won't find someone here better suited for him?"

"What did I just tell ye about talking yerself out of it," she frowned and swatted her daughter on the behind with a wooden spoon. County Cork coming out on her tongue and in her hand.

"Did you really just spank me? Mother, I am thirty-three! Corporal punishment has fallen out of fashion you know?"

"Not in this house it hasn't and don't change the subject. He hasn't found anyone here yet has he? No. He has chosen you, my darling. And why shouldn't he? You're beautiful, funny, and smart as a whip. You're a stubborn ass but, that can't be avoided really. I know who your father is," she added with a wink.

Carefully pouring the last ladle full of coddle into the white stone serving crock and handing it to the serving girl who had been waiting patiently, bored to death of the woes of the family Patrick no doubt.

"There we are. Thank you, Lucy be careful not to spill that on yourself it's very hot."

"Aye ma'am," the blonde servant nodded at her employer. Teagan picked up on a familiar person approaching her house just as Lucy was exiting the kitchen.

"Stand up straight," Bryan McCarthy snapped at his sons as they made their way up the winding driveway. Both boys straightened their backs in response.

"Matthew, can't you do anything about that hair," he barked exasperatedly, "Rylan, fix your tie!"

"Father, please relax," Rylan asked quietly, straightening his tie as he did so.

"Yes, please. You really are making too big a deal of this."

"I have known these Folk since we were all sprites. A big enough deal cannot be made of this!"

"You are driving me to drink old man and it isn't even six o'clock yet," Rylan fired back at his father, shaking his head. Matthew attempted poorly to stifle his laughter with a cough and looked down to watch his step on the uneven ground.

"Very well then, do not be disrespectful," Bryan clucked, his mustache bristling as he took a deep breath to steady his nerves.

"Aye sir," Rylan responded, rolling his eyes. He picked up his pace to catch up with his brother who was apparently in a hurry to see his lover. Matthew was humming the lyrics to 'The Irish Rover' as they went. His brother joined him as they approached the house, leaving their neurotic father in their wake.

She hummed the familiar tune to herself as she landed hard on the ground just outside the wood line of their back yard. Setting glamour about them in case there were any unwanted visitors, she made her way to the house as quickly as her body would allow. She stopped at the edge of the stone pathway that led to the back door and fell to her knees as she saw familiar faces securing the perimeter, their armed guard was already here. She exhaled heavily and withdrew her magic, revealing herself and Rylan to her fellow officers. Two of them ran immediately to her side, each taking a McCarthy in their arms and carrying them inside. The last thing Teagan remembered was hearing her Sergeant barking commands at his subordinates and seeing blood start to issue from Rylan's nose.

Fight

There are four possible responses in the brain when confronted with attack; Fight, flight, posture and submit. He chose to fight readily.

He had seen Blair barreling toward them looking possessed and had acted on instinct. Teagan would be furious but at least she would be alive. If it was bait they wanted, bait he would be and they could try their damnedest to get to him as long as they left his family alone. If it was information they wanted, whoever Blair was working for, they would not get it from him. Who would come after them he couldn't say, there wasn't anyone left alive from the war to come after him and any Fae that had participated would know better than to come after him because of the family he'd been lucky enough to marry into. Teagan may have made some enemies during the course of her duties but, none who would be at a Faerie run hospital and again none stupid enough to come after royalty unless someone was hell bent on a coup.

How Blair managed to get involved in a hit on his wife's sister was beyond him but, it was definitely his brother-in-law he saw, Rylan assured himself. So now he waited. He waited and blocked Teagan out lest she get drawn further into whatever business they'd suddenly found themselves part of. He had taken on the role of protector the moment he met Teagan though truthfully, she hardly needed protecting. She was strong, fierce and endlessly intelligent. She would be terrifying if he didn't love and respect her so much. She had never really known, because he never told her, how much her spirit pulled him through his darkest hours when he was fighting overseas. That's the thing about Teagan Patrick that sets her apart, you don't have her, she has you. Rylan had only met a Queen once, when his parents entertained the idea of sending he and Matthew away to another court, but Teagan carried herself the same Queenly way; Self-possessed, brooding and beyond clever. Teagan was right to admonish him before he left to fight a war that really wasn't his to fight but, his stubbornness outweighed his logic and he went anyway. He went and she waited. She lived her life and waited for him to return. She never gave up on him even when he had given up on himself, she was steadfast to her core. Another thing he loved about her. He was very aware that she was trying desperately to crack into his thoughts and he very much needed her to remain 'in the dark' for her safety as much as his own, if whoever attacked them was able to infiltrate his mind, they'd have a hidden route to her and he would never forgive himself. My steadfast and tenacious love take a break. Rest. Breathe. Eat for goodness sake, eat because you're eating for two! Our boy has no idea yet, how loved he is and how anxiously we are awaiting him. He has no idea the world that will greet him, the family who will welcome him and the legacy he will continue. He will be great, whoever he is, and I cannot wait to continue growing our family.

Seek

Rylee and the rest of the pediatrics nurses had dressed up as leprechauns in honor of Saint Patrick's Day that weekend; 1800's green velvet dress, petticoat included, and shoulder length auburn wig were a bad choice. The kids enjoyed their authentic costumes but, it was heavy and hot, and Rylee was grateful the day was nearly done. No wonder she had so many siblings; if this attire was fashionable when she was young and newlywed, she'd have been naked as often as possible too.

Because of the shifts they worked, the crew that worked Monday through Thursday had Friday, Saturday and half of Sunday off; Rylee was the only day shift nurse left until her Midnight shift counterpart arrived and relieved her in about an hour. She looked up from her nearly finished final chart of the day to check on the two rooms across from the station where she was standing, that's another thing about petticoats; one could never find a comfortable sitting position while wearing one. Aden, her patient in room 4, was finally sleeping soundly; he had been admitted the week before with iron poisoning. A human neighbor had given him chocolate chip cookies for a snack when he and her son had come in from playing; she neglected to check the ingredients list of the baking powder fully and it contained aluminum, not lethal for human children.

He had been closer to death than life when Sadee ran him to her from the emergency room door where his father arrived with him as she was leaving to go home for lunch.

He couldn't remember anything, not his name, not his birthday, not even his most loved comfort blanket. He could still recognize color though and had slurred 'pink' when Rylee had asked him about her scrubs. They had put him on oxygen before he lost consciousness and pumped him full of fluids; saline to rehydrate him and an infusion of lavender sugar to counter act the iron. The extremities of his six-year-old body twitched and his voice was naught but, a screech for three days. On the fourth day his lungs found a steady rhythm, his throat hoarse from screaming had found some relief in his silence. Last night his limbs had ceased convulsing and early this afternoon his jaw relaxed its clench. Iron was not a thing to be trifled with where Faeries were concerned.

Drew, her other charge, had chosen Peter Pan as his afternoon movie and "The Crocodile Theme" had gotten stuck in her head. She hummed this while double checking that all her charts were signed when an acrid smell wafting down the hallway from the East Wing tickled her nose, the lights began to flicker and dim before going out altogether. She quickly checked that protection runes were in order over all the patients' doors, closed and then locked each in turn. When she reached the last one, Aden's door, she heard a boom and what sounded like the earth cracking from the same direction the smell had come, it was suddenly very hot and loud.

She heard screams and saw several of her coworkers on the

other side of the glass wall that separated North and South areas of the East wing; running, flying, pushing, punching, and tripping over each other to get to the exits. Smoke billowed behind them and started to creep under the door at the opposite end of the hallway where she stood paralyzed by indecision; she couldn't abandon the children but, she couldn't just stand there either. She forced herself to move toward the screams, moving robotically at first and then barely quicker than a walk. She kept her eyes and ears peeled for any sign of movement or, further sounds of danger. Then she saw him, entering the South side of the East Wing from the North was Blair Davies. Walking at a strange gait and pace, she realized he had been injured and was limping. She quickened forward to help him but stopped midstride when he looked up through the smoke and they locked eyes; he was wild, animalistic, possessed. She realized he had caused this panic and devastation. She took a deep breath, hiked her skirts and rushed him.

"Rylee," he barked at her.

She ignored him and kept running.

"If you stop now, I will spare you, darling," he hissed, dragging a blade he had drawn from his belt against the brick wall.

"Oh I doubt that," she responded breathlessly as she ducked under his arm and made for the exit behind him.

"Stop and I will spare the children," he laughed as she pushed the door open and made an about face to follow her, picking up speed as he did.

"You will not touch them," she stopped just before going

through the door and glared back at him, her ginger wig askew on her head.

"Don't count on it," he growled.

"You've got to be fucking kidding me. This cannot be happening," she thought. The smoke had fully engulfed the hallway between the North and South areas of the East Wing and was rapidly overtaking the Maternity Wing entirely. Taking shallow breaths through her mouth to avoid inhaling too much smoke, she kept her head down as she ran to keep her vision as clear as possible. She heard the labored breathing and heavy footfalls of her injured pursuer behind her as she ran blindly through the dark of the hospital, her faerie senses guiding her through the destruction.

Sliding on blood and she dared not think what else as she hastened toward the entrance, she tripped twice over bodies she was sure she would recognize in the daylight; they were not prepared for what had happened that day. No amount of drilling can teach you how to handle the adrenaline rush that pushes logic aside. Your brain switches to auto pilot, that fight or flight reflex kicks in and it's every Fae for them self. She saw a streak of scarlet hair fly upward near the main entrance and was immediately sick to her stomach. "Please," she prayed, "Fiona please don't let it have been one of my baby sisters."

Blair tripped and fell over the same bodies her feet had found; buying her just enough time to make her own escape out the front door without him seeing which way she would go. She moved as quickly as she could; saying another prayer to the mother of them all that she had been enough of a distraction to her brother-in-law and that her protection runes would hold until she could get back to her sprites where they lay healing.

The cool air was fresh, and her lungs welcomed it greedily; she headed North and then West to her parents' home. She would be safe there for sure and her father would know what to do.

She stopped and turned when she had put enough distance between herself and the hospital to do so; black smoke permeated the sky above her workplace, she saw red and blue flashing lights approaching and her fellow Folk looked like ants escaping their hill from where she had stopped to catch her breath. Tears started streaming down her cheeks and blurred her vision when she turned back to finish her flight home; it had never seemed to take so long before and she checked ahead often to make sure she was still on the correct course.

Arriving at her parents' gate after what seemed like an eternity of running, she picked up her skirts and went inside without knocking on the front door. Slamming it shut behind her, she called twice for her mother; when she received no response, she breathed deeply to steady her nerves and quietly set about searching the house. It had already been decorated for the evening's festivities; clover strewn about the gleaming counters that were waiting patiently for the heavily laden food containers they would hold later; little faerie doors and green men set about in various old hiding places her mother always used. She was comforted by the familiar smells of cherry tobacco and soda bread but, was wound as tightly as the coil of a brand-new Jack in the Box; prepared to spring at the slightest indication of movement.

She found her mother at the back of the house; Rose Patrick was a blur of dark hair and white denim as she bustled about taking care of the list of things her King had left her to do.

"Mother," Rylee whispered from the doorway.

"My stars you startled me," she yelped, clutching the red cloth of her t shirt over her heart.

"I called for you twice from the front door."

"I am sorry dear I am in an awful hurry and can't hear much but, my own thoughts."

"Here," she handed Rylee a large leather satchel, "hold this open for me."

"Mother what's going on? I was at work when Blair attacked the hospital. He threatened the sprites, he threatened me," her voice high with emotion.

"I know. Your father is on his way to Teagan's, she and Rylan were attacked," she stopped for the first time since beginning the list of things her husband had asked her to do.

"No. Oh no, no, no, no, no," Rylee started crying again and slumped onto her parents perfectly made bed, leather satchel limp in her hands.

"We haven't time to crumble peanut, get up now our family needs us," her mother nudged her.

"Here," Rylee handed her mother the half full leather bag, "I'll be right back."

She jogged the short distance down the hall to Teagan's old room. Their mother had knocked down the wall between hers and Meagan's rooms when the two had decided they wanted to share; it had long been a playroom for her nieces and nephews complete with all the Patrick children's old toys.

She threw open the large cedar wood toy box in the middle of the back wall designated for the "girl" toys and dug almost all the way to the bottom before she found what she was looking for. Hugging Josephine to her chest tightly, she ran back to her parents' room to finish helping her mother.

"Here," she put it on top of all the other items and pulled the top shut, "for Teagan."

"For Teagan," her mother nodded.

"What else," Rylee asked, wiping tears off her cheeks.

"You need to change," her mother suggested, helping the already sideways wig off her head.

"Yes ma'am," she let her mother lead her back to her old room where some of her old things had been kept. She took a pair of black scrubs from the back, clean under things from one of the dresser drawers and headed to the bathroom to clean up.

She splashed water on her soot-streaked face and freed her wet with sweat hair from its pins before changing; putting her dirty costume in the hamper, she found her mother waiting for her in the hall.

"What happened to them? How bad are they?"

"I don't know yet. We are headed to their house soon though."

"Soon? Why aren't we going straight there?"

"We need to check on everyone else before, it's what your father and I decided. He would go straight to Teagan's as she asked, and I would check on the rest of our family."

"I'm glad I came here then; I'd hate you to go alone."

"That's the spirit, let's go," Rose smiled at her daughter reassuringly, she took her hand and led them out the front door.

Her own apartment that she shared with her twin was their first stop. They didn't bother with knocking and as Rylee hadn't had time to fetch her keys after the attack, along with everything else she had taken to work, they just kicked in the front door, her brother Travis would have to put his carpentry skills to work later.

"What the bloody hell is this all about," Sadee fumed after the dust had settled and she saw who had broken and entered. They had caught her fresh from the shower and she clutched the front of her towel while they filled her in, blonde hair a tangled mess and dripping onto their blue suede couch.

"Get dried and dressed then dear and we'll all be off," their mother instructed.

"Aye ma'am," Sadee replied robotically, still too shocked to muster any real emotion just yet.

Rylee went to the kitchen to procure a snack while they waited for what seemed like an hour, after refusing sustenance herself, her mother assured her Sadee had only been about three minutes and would not take much longer.

"Indeed," her twin reappeared from her bedroom, "the perks of having short hair, I can get ready in a hurry if need be."

"Are you seriously wearing yoga gear," Rylee judged Sadee's fitted grey hoodie and black yoga leggings.

"Are you seriously worried about my fashion right now," Sadee rebuffed her sister's judgment, standing next to her while she slipped on her well-worn flats.

"Girls please behave, we have a busy evening, and I don't want any fuss from you two," Rose Patrick sighed admonishment at them like they were ten years old.

"Here," Rylee handed Sadee a granola bar, "you'll need it."

"Thanks," she ripped it open and ate it hurriedly as they left through what use to be their front door, Rose set an enchantment to keep unwanted beings out.

Their next stop was The McCarthy's or, what the family referred to as 'Triple M Ranch.' Matt and Meagan lived on the west side of Tucson on a beautiful ten-acre ranch outfitted with a horse barn and pasture, they only kept four horses but, Rylee was sure they were the best kept equines who had ever lived. The McCarthy land was massive and very well-tended by the myriad hands that staffed the place, Matthew was the horse lover and his wife wanted as little to keep up in the way of his hobby as possible.

She held the inside of their home to an almost museum standard of cleanliness, however and prided herself on doing so all on her own; she hated the idea of anyone but herself cleaning up after she and her husband. The three Patrick ladies spread out to check the property for any intruders or signs of struggle. Meeting at the large carved oak front door once they were satisfied all was well, Rose picked the lock and they entered slowly, clearing each room as they made their way to the back. They found a very surprised and half-dressed Meagan McCarthy making dinner in her spacious kitchen; Matt made his appearance from the back of the house whistling as he entered the kitchen, covering his cotton boxer brief clothed lower half with his hands when he saw who was there.

"Glad you're putting that apron to good use," Rose nodded at Meagan, somehow managing to keep a straight face. The twins lost all sense of decorum and were laughing heartily at their siblings.

"So sorry to interrupt you two but, we have an emergency," Rylee laughed behind her hand.

"Yes, we do," Rose turned her gaze to her son in law, "I think pants might be a good idea, Matthew."

This was met with another round of laughter from all of her daughters this time.

"I'm not sure what you're giggling about Meagan Leigh. You'll need more than that bit of apron to cover your ass, so get a move on and we'll explain once everyone is a bit more decent," she instructed, eyebrow raised.

"I don't know how you kept a straight face that whole time!"

"I almost lost it when you two started," Rose giggled with her twins, "I do hope they had gotten at least one round in."

"Gross," Rylee wrinkled her nose.

"How else am I to get grandchildren then," she asked through her laughter.

"It would help if you interrupted less," Sadee barely got out through her breathless giggle fit and snorted once she had, Rylee was in stitches again as well.

"Goodness," Rose inhaled deeply, wiping a tear from her eye with her leather gloved hand and laughing less enthusiastically, "I needed that, thank you."

"Well, what is it," an annoyed but, more appropriately dressed Meagan had reappeared in her kitchen, "Sadee did you just come from yoga? Thanks for the invite."

"Really right now? You were just trying to make a baby in your kitchen, don't bother yourself about my attire."

"I said you looked an idiot."

"Sit down Rua Mion, this one's a doozy," Rose advised her youngest once her husband, having found a shirt as well as pants, had joined them.

After getting them up to speed, Matt remained standing and massaged his wife's shoulders while they listened, the ever-growing group were off to Travis' house next, determined to protect kith and kin.

Pause

She had fought them, even in her unconscious state, they told him.

"She wouldn't let us touch her," Officer Henley informed him, angry red wounds that looked suspiciously like finger-nail scratches ran down the right side of his face. Looking like a scalded dog behind his mirrored sunglasses, "She won't leave his side."

"Of course not," King Patrick reassured him, shaking his head and smiling sadly; "she is stubborn like her father." He removed his rimless aviators, leather flying jacket and gloves and set them on the table in the entryway before taking the long walk down the hall to his daughter's bedroom. Officer Henley led him to Officer Galen Murphy, who he recognized as Rylan's best friend, standing astride the open door. There were Officers stationed outside each window and several others standing post at various stations throughout the property; he practically had to give blood before they were satisfied he was who he claimed to be, the officers exchanged pleasantries and necessary information allowing him to pass.

She was on the floor near the bed when he strode in, boots as heavy on the polished cement floor as his heart felt in his chest; *'She would kill me for not taking off my boots,'* he silently chastised himself.

Her limbs were at odd angles, awkward and uncomfortable looking. He scooped her up, scarlet hair spilling over his arm. Her green eyes open wide, unseeing, swollen and crusted with tears. He carefully carried her to the large worn leather high backed chair next to Rylan's side of the bed. Removing the few articles of clothing his son in law had set there, he gingerly sat down taking care not to agitate what he assumed was a Feandragoon though, it had been ages since he'd seen one so could not be sure. He sent calming energy her way and projected who he was and why he was there, hoping she would pick up what he was sending out; one or, the other worked because she perched on the back of the chair and only eyed him suspiciously until Teagan relaxed.

Cradling her like he had so many times when she was young, his favorite who almost didn't make it, she was late the doctors said. Though, he would learn later that she always did things on her own time. He smiled down at her as this thought crossed his mind, wondering if she was aware of his thoughts even now. Doctor Benjamin had given her only seventy-two hours to live. She was sick, underweight and had abnormal brain scans. She was also stubborn. She was here and she had no intention of an early curtain call. He was grateful for that, especially after Liam. She fought the iron poisoning that had occurred in utero, one of his enemies attacked his pregnant Queen.

They were both healed nearly as soon as it happened but, couldn't be sure Teagan was one hundred percent until she was born. She was attended to by the best healers and would put on three pounds in the three days after she arrived.

At dusk on the third day, Teagan Patrick opened sage green eyes she had inherited from her father and smiled at him as he held her, eyes closed in silent prayer. She moved her wings down toward the forearm supporting her spine and watched his face intently. He smiled and snuggled her close as she began to beat her wings as steadily as her limited motor skills would allow. He relaxed entirely when she let loose for the first time the mischievous giggle that would never cease to melt his heart.

Teagan rested heavily upon her father's forearm, the same that had supported her for days after her belated birth and countless times after. She breathed in his familiar scent, earth, leather and cherry vanilla Cavendish. Dad smell. She closed her eyes and relaxed. She knew she was safe and that her father was thinking of her beginning. She plucked up a memory they could both appreciate; the first time Teagan stood up for herself and began to use her voice at her father's behest.

"Oh, come on Teagan it's just a doll, you can share," Sadee teased her little sister. Rylee and Teagan had been playing tug of war with Teagan's most loved doll for a good ten minutes and neither was willing to budge. The eight-year-old twins were not bullies separately but, together were unwavering in their mission for toy domination in the Patrick household.

"Yeah, come on Tea, just give up already," Rylee grunted, nearly ripping the red-haired baby doll's right arm out of its socket.

Shoulders drooping resignedly, the four-year-old gave in to her twin sisters' demands and the dolls left arm hung limply in midair as Rylee almost fell on her backside from the backlash of pulling so hard.

Exchanging an identical look of cruel triumph the twins turned and ran to their shared room, adding Teagan's beloved baby doll to their growing hoard. She silently bid Josephine adieu and left to find her father, making her way down the hall from the playroom to the Patrick patriarch's outdoor work space, her left hand tucked in the pocket of her short sleeved grey tunic dress, trailing the fingers of her right hand along the vivid green paint on the wall. She rounded the corner, and her favorite person came into view. Her athair was sitting in his chair, smoking his pipe and writing in his notebook. He loved writing down his thoughts and writing poems. She pushed the door open and ran across the small patch of grass to sit in his lap.

He lifted his notebook in the air so his four-year-old daughter wouldn't hit her head on it as she pulled herself up into his lap. He exhaled the smoke from his lungs in a loud chuckle at the sullen look on her face.

"Oh, now rua, what's wrong?"

'Rylee and Sadee' Teagan thought at him.

"What about them?"

'Mean,' he heard in his head.

If anyone were listening, they would've been convinced the old man had lost his marbles and was talking to himself. Outside their family and his childhood friend Trinity, no one knew of Teagan's ability. Even they weren't sure yet of how far reaching it really was.

Trinity was slowly working it out. Testing her gradually so as not to traumatize the sprite.

"Use your words Teagan."

'I am.'

"Out loud, please."

'It won't matter.'

"You must verbalize what you need."

'Why?'

"Not everyone will be able to 'hear' you always and you need to get used to speaking out loud."

'Why?'

"You are gifted my dear but, not everyone is and it's possible that we can all 'hear' you because we share blood. We aren't quite sure yet exactly how your gift works."

'Trinity can hear me.'

"Yes because she is special too."

'If someone can't hear me, maybe they don't need to know what I have to say.'

"Aye rua, you are a stubborn little cuss," he said laughing heartily.

'Just like you,' she stuck her tongue out at him.

"You need to stand up for yourself Teagan Inez. You can't just give up when you're outnumbered or, when things get tough."

'I know but, they are bigger and meaner than me.'

Resting his cheek against her furrowed forehead he began rocking their chair back and forth, hugging her closer to his chest.

"You don't have to get mean to get what you need. Reason with them, you are a logical sprite and so are they."

'I'm not so sure about them.'

"Come now, don't be catty. What exactly did they do? Tell me out loud."

Teagan took a few deep breaths and looked up into her father's green eyes, a mirror image of her own, "They took Josephine."

"See now that wasn't so hard was it? Why did they take her? Out loud again, please."

"Because I was playing with her and they wanted her," her tiny voice said slowly.

"Did they ask you to share?"

'No.'

"Out loud Teagan."

"No, sir they didn't," she huffed, rolling her eyes.

"So what are you going to do about it?"

"Steal her back after they've gone to bed."

"That is a clever idea but, why don't you try a more direct approach."

'Like what?'

"Out. Loud. Teagan Inez," he said sternly.

"Like what?"

"Ask them to give it back."

"What?"

"That got your attention now didn't it," he laughed.

"What do you mean ask them? What if they refuse?"

"Then they refuse and you come get me but, you have to try on your own first little one."

"I'm nervous to ask."

"Asking doesn't hurt anything rua. If you never ask, you will never know and knowing is a very important thing."

"Knowing what?"

"Anything! Everything! Knowledge is the most important tool you can have in your arsenal."

"Arsenal?"

"I'll explain more of that later but, for now just go ask your sisters to give Josephine back."

"If I do, what will you do for me?"

"I see your siblings have taught you how to negotiate. What would you want?"

"What are you willing to offer me?"

"If you ask, I will give you a necco wafer. If you get her back, I will give you a whole pack of necco wafers."

"Chocolate ones?"

"Aye ma'am, chocolate ones."

"Deal," she said holding out her hand to shake on their agreement. He took her little hand in his and shook on the first of many negotiations they would conduct over the years. She hopped down, adjusted the dark green tights keeping the cool spring air from her legs and made her way slowly toward the house, thinking of what she would say the entire way to the twins' bedroom door. She raised a white knuckled fist and knocked gingerly on the black lacquered cherry wood door.

"Who is it," Sadee called.

"It's Teagan," she responded and heard the shock going through their minds that she spoke out loud.

"What do you want rua," Sadee asked, still refusing to open the door.

"I want Josephine back. Please," she asked at the door.

"No," the twins said in unison, giggling at Teagan's request. She could hear them thinking of evil things to do to her doll and decided to ask politely one more time before going in to save her.

"Please give her back? She was my Winter Solstice present from athair," she plead with her sisters.

"Why should we give her back Tea?"

"Because she is mine."

"Not good enough," they laughed mischievously.

"Fine. Either you give her to me or, I am coming in after her. You will not drown her in the creek or, use her for firewood!"

"Good luck getting in the door little one, it's locked."

Closing her eyes, Teagan inhaled deeply. When she exhaled she blew the air at the door handle and saw it clicking open in her mind's eye. With a small pop, the door opened slightly and she pushed her way inside. Greeted by her sister's shocked faces and Sadee redressing Josephine in a hideous pink tutu, she took advantage of their inability to move and snatched Josephine from her hand. Turning on her heel and running for the hall, she slammed the door shut behind her using her thoughts. The weekly lessons she had with Lady Trinity were paying off and she couldn't wait to tell her father.

Nearly bowling her brother Travis over in her haste to get outdoors, she tripped. Josephine went flying across the living room and ended up under the sofa, her tights now had a large tear in the right knee.

"Geez Teagan slow down," Travis reprimanded, scowling at her.

"Sorry," she said aloud, adding yet another stunned sibling to her list. She scrambled to get up and wondered why her sisters hadn't given chase yet. Scooping her doll from under the couch and checking her tender knee, she also checked in mentally with her sisters. She found they were still frozen where they sat playing and couldn't speak either. Now very concerned, Teagan hurried to get outside.

"Athair! Athair," she called as she approached her father, still scratching away in his notebook, his pipe on the table beside him.

"Ah I see you rescued Josephine. Did negotiations go smoothly then," he asked producing his promised pack of chocolate Necco wafers seemingly from nowhere.

"No. I think I hurt Sadee and Rylee," breathless from the run and pushing her hair from her eyes.

"What do you mean rua," he asked, setting down his notebook.

"I mean they wouldn't let me in or, give me my doll so I used my mind to unlock the door and I think they're frozen," her words seemed to come out all at the same time and she was glad she could show her father what she meant. Slowly rising from his chair, he took Teagan's hand and led her back into the house where her sisters sat seemingly frozen in time.

"Hmm...Teagan, what exactly were you thinking of when you opened the door and took Josephine?"

"I was thinking that I wanted the door to open and I wanted Sadee and Rylee not to chase me."

"I see...did you think of them being stuck or, frozen?"

"Yes, I wanted them to be stuck where they were."

"Think of them being unstuck."

"Athair?"

"Think of them being able to move normally. Think of them going back to playing just as they were before."

Teagan closed her eyes and did as she was asked. Letting go the air she had gulped in an effort to relax, she opened her eyes to see her sisters a bit confused but playing with their own dolls as they were before.

"What are you doing in here Tea? We didn't invite you, get out rua," Rylee spat at her sister.

"Is that my tutu on Josephine? Next time ask, please," an exasperated Sadee glowered at her younger sister.

"Girls be kind to your sister. You took her doll, she was just taking it back."

"Yes athair. Sorry Teagan," they unconvincingly replied in unison.

Timothy Patrick picked up his frightened child, ruefully holding her doll and they headed to the living room.

"I think we had better fetch Trinity," he told her, his eyes clouded with worry.

'Lady Trinity,' Teagan reached for the elf's mind with her own.

'Teagan! How can I be of service darling,' came the reply nearly instantly.

'I did something bad! Meet in the grove.'

'On my way.'

'She is on her way to the grove athair,' Teagan informed her father.

"Ah my little rua, do not shut down now! You didn't do anything wrong, we just need to know exactly what it was you did," he said reassuringly and kissed her forehead as they walked to the back yard.

Teagan rested her head against her father's shoulder and clutched his shirt for dear life as they passed the fountain at the edge of their patio. He strode down the stone pathway toward the large forest that lay behind their home. It took them fifteen minutes to get to their meeting place, about a mile and a half into the trees from the edge of their yard.

He set Teagan down gingerly and crouched so his face was directly in front of hers.

He took her little chin between the finger and thumb of his right hand and said, "You must understand you did nothing wrong or, bad Teagan Inez. You used your gift and that is never wrong or, bad. We just need to make sure you know how to utilize it properly alright."

'Aye sir,' she replied, forcing an unsure half smile.

"Don't be nervous, Lady Trinity will help."

At that, the elf appeared from the south through the fog. Pulling back the dark green hood of her long cloak, she shook her long dark hair free and walked straight for Teagan; deep purple eyes catching the young faerie's nervous gaze.

'Hello Princess Teagan.'

'Hello Lady Trinity.'

'There is no need to be frightened child, just breathe. Your father is trying very hard to calm you with his own gift. Let it take effect.'

'Aye ma'am,' Teagan replied relaxing her mind. She was immediately flooded with her father's calming energy. It was almost too much and she nearly curled up for a nap right there amongst the trees.

"Pull it back a bit Sir, we don't want her to go comatose," Trinity's quiet voice trickled through the atmosphere.

"My apologies," he replied, dialing down his energy.

'Thank you,' Teagan yawned widely.

"Now, let's all use our voices alright?"

"Alright," Teagan nodded agreement. She quickly explained what she had done, her father filling in what she missed and describing more completely what her four year old tongue could not articulate. Trinity absorbed their story with a furrowed brow and thought on it for what seemed to Teagan like an eternity.

"It sounds to me like she manipulated their environment, paused time for them for a moment. Teagan, you promised you wouldn't try that without me just yet," she admonished her young student.

"I didn't mean to break my promise. I did not realize that's what I was doing. I was just trying to save Josephine and they were being so unreasonable," she pouted.

"I understand that but, just because someone is being unreasonable doesn't mean we can force them to do something they don't want to do. Because of the powerful gift you have it is very important to try our best to manage our emotions."

"Alright. I'm sorry," a deflated Teagan grumbled at the ground.

"That was a very interesting use of your gift though. You remembered how to undo it as well. I am disappointed that you did not keep your word but, I am proud of you for putting our lessons to good use," Trinity beamed at her.

"I am sorry Lady Trinity and thank you very much," she grinned up at the elf.

"If that's it then, I think we'll be off. She'll be here for her lesson on Wednesday," King Patrick scooped up his sprite in one arm and embraced his father's former advisor with the other.

"Go easy on her, she is still learning but, she has a good heart and I'm sure no harm will be done by her."

"Thank you. Journey safely home friend."

"And you as well My Lord," Trinity nodded and pulled her hood back over her head, turning southward through the fog to wherever she lived when she wasn't teaching Teagan in the woods of Bansalee.

Teagan brought them both back to the present as the king wiped a tear from his cheek.

'Come back to us my rua, when you're ready come back and remember your words.'

'Not yet Athair. Not yet. Just five more minutes.'

VAMPIRE

Vampire

The King shifted slightly where he sat still cradling his child, Teagan stirred gently, still asleep in his arms as she had been all afternoon with Airioch camped on the back of the chair keeping watch over them all. Sergeant Murphy stepped to the threshold of the room just then and cleared his throat as quietly as he could.

"Sir, there is a Maeve Stewart here to see you. She is on the approved list of visitors but, we wanted to clear it with you before letting her through."

"Thank you, Maeve is always welcome in my family's home."

The Sergeant nodded understanding and turned to escort their visitor back.

'Rua, Maeve is here for you.'

'Very well athair. Just let me sleep a moment more.'

His daughter's longtime friend stepped tenuously through the doorway and came to sit on the floor at the King's feet. Airioch snorted disapproval and began to pace, he was unsure whether or, not she could understand him but he tried to assuage her anxiety as best he could.

'She is only half vampire,' he thought, *'Fuil Leannan.'*

It must have translated at least partially because the Fe-andragoon quit pacing, her narrowed gaze never left Maeve's general vicinity though. The holes in the knees of the half Faeries blue jeans reflected the mood everyone would carry today. Her fitted red long sleeved Henley screamed comfort, a thing none of them would have for a very long while. She took Teagan's hand in hers and spoke as quietly as she had entered. This was an easy thing as the half vampire Faerie was scared for her friends and she dared not speak above a whisper lest her fear betray her. She rested her forehead on their hands, her long yellow hair spilling about either side of her face hiding it from view.

"Do we know anything yet My Lord?"

"We know some things. Do not be offended that I won't share them with you."

"No sir. Are they okay?"

"No. They have been as you see them since this afternoon. Rylan is unresponsive and Teagan is conscious but, only just."

"What can I do?"

"Share with her. Let her know you are here. She would like that."

"Aye sir."

Teagan knew Maeve was there, she felt her before her father had announced her presence. She reached out to her friends mind and immersed them in a memory they were both fond of; The Arizona desert 1919 was a place they both remembered quite well.

Maeve Stewart had been friends with Teagan Patrick since sprite hood and they considered each other family. Teagan had come home from Ireland a different tween and spent many a night in various seedy establishments attempting to stave off her melancholy. This particular night, Maeve went looking for her at King Patrick's request and she found her charge at El Jefe's; a less than savory bar nestled in Agua Prieta, Mexico just a few miles away from their home in Douglas, Arizona. The men who frequented El Jefe's were mostly ranchers and cattlemen. When she was not there, she could be found at the Gadsden; which was frequented by affluent gentlemen who employed those frequenting El Jefe's.

Elegant and statuesque, tonight Maeve wore a low cut dress the color of canary feathers that matched her perfectly curled waist length hair which she had pinned delicately at the nape of her neck. Her large turquoise eyes scanned the dirty, poorly lit bar for the shell who once was her friend.

"Ah que pajaro bonita," the short, portly bar tender exclaimed as Maeve located Teagan on her usual bar stool in front of the bar.

"Esta mi amiga preferente, Adriana," Teagan nodded in Maeve's direction. Wonderful, Maeve thought, we are using aliases tonight.

"Hola Inez!Como estas," Maeve asked over the exuberant band playing loudly in the corner.

"Muy bien, Muy bien, gracias," Teagan yelled as she drained the last of the tequila sitting in front of her. Fiona help me, Maeve sighed inwardly, this is going to be a long night.

"Senor! Diez mas tequilas por favor," Teagan requested of the bar tender. Turning to Maeve she said conspiratorially, "You need to catch up." Exhaling quietly Maeve thought, its going to be a very, very long night. Taking two cigarettes from her silver and ivory case, she lit both and handed Teagan one.

"Ah gracias amor," Teagan thanked her before taking a long drag and exhaling slowly. It was one of few things that brought her friend joy these days; feeling the fire fill her lungs and the smoke caress her tongue.

She had told her this much a few weeks prior on a night almost identical to this one. Teagan was a woman of few words lately. Tequila and cigarettes aside, she didn't know what brought her friend joy. Since coming home from Ireland, she had been cold, shut off, she didn't even "listen" anymore and refused to tell Maeve why.

"Necco wafers. Chocolate ones," Teagan slurred already eight tequilas in.

"Okay," a perplexed Maeve responded.

"You were thinking you don't know what makes me happy. I don't really know either but, I like Necco wafers. Chocolate ones."

"What happened in Ireland?"

"Tequilas senioritas," the bar tender returned jubilantly with their drinks.

"Gracias senor! Quiero botea aqui, por favor." Eyes as big as saucers, the little man left to get what was left of their bottle of tequila.

"Y sal y limones por favor," Teagan yelled after him as he shook his head in response.

Teagan downed her two shots consecutively as Maeve began catching up.

Finishing her cigarette in silence while Maeve did the same with her tequila, Teagan pondered what to tell her friend in answer to her question. Taking a deep breath and extinguishing the last of it, the liquor had begun to take its affect and she began solemnly "Everyone thinks I drink because I'm sad. I don't. I drink to go numb. I drink so I don't have to feel anything at all. I drink to drown out the voices...his voice."

"Meggs said she had never seen you so content."

Their bar tender had returned with their bottle and began to clean up all but, two glasses in front of them. Nodding thanks at the attentive service, lighting two more cigarettes and handing one to Maeve, Teagan told her "I let him in."

Nearly choking on tequila and smoke, Maeve coughed and tried quietly to recover from shock.

"Yeah. He said he was in love with me and then he left. He left to fight a war that isn't even ours." She took another drag and poured them each another shot.

"He didn't even ask how I felt about it. He just enlisted and now I don't know if he will ever be back."

"I'm sorry," Maeve uttered quietly, clinking her glass against Teagan's; each taking their respective shots and pouring two more.

"I let him in. Actually, he just showed up and I had to fight to keep him out. He didn't even push, he was just...there and now I can't get him out, unless I drown him in adult beverages."

"So, we drink," Maeve clinked their glasses in cheers again and each drained their tequila in one gulp.

"We drink," Teagan smiled mischievously. "Enough sadness, we have your birthday to plan! Thirty-four. It's a big one! No longer a sprite, finally a tween," she winked at Maeve.

"Ah me, thirty-four! I'm glad you went first," Maeve chuckled exhaling a puff of smoke before stamping out the butt of her cigarette and pouring them each another drink.

"So, I'm thinking an extravagant party at The Gadsden or, we could head up to Tombstone and give that little town some color," Teagan suggested, emptying her glass and finishing her smoke.

"Tombstone I think," Maeve decided thoughtfully, "I haven't seen Morgan in a whole month of Sundays!"

"Indeed. The Earp's have always been good for a bit of excitement," Teagan concurred. Standing slowly to ensure they kept their balance, Teagan paid for their drinks and grabbed the nearly empty bottle of tequila by the handle as the well lubricated Faeries stumbled out onto the dusty street. Leaning on each other for support and stopping only to light more cigarettes, they made a steady pace toward home. They heard footsteps approaching quickly behind them about a mile or so.

"He's harmless," Teagan feeling Maeve tense up.

"I'm hungry," she said seriously, her eyes flashing. Baring her razor-sharp teeth in a murderous smile, Maeve turned and breathed the scent of the stranger longingly into her lungs.

"Make it quick and clean," Teagan warned. She continued the journey north as Maeve disappeared from her side. It wouldn't take long, it never did. The first time Teagan had seen her friend eat a human, they were eight years old, and she was horrified.

It was the first time Teagan had truly been afraid of anything. Her parents explained to her that because Maeve's father, Maxwell, was vampire and her mother, Gwen, was Fae; Maeve was Blood Lover or, as they preferred in their native Gaelic: 'Fuil Leannan.' She would not survive on food, only blood could sustain her. They explained that her mother would teach Maeve how to use her Faerie magic to ease the passing of her prey and her father would make sure she knew how to be discreet. As they learned about her dual nature together, Maeve helped Teagan understand that most Fuil Leannan did not hate humans. It was quite the opposite in fact, she quite loved humans in the same way Teagan loved bananas or, steak. Maeve had a great respect for humans as their life sustained hers and she was careful to always make their passing as comfortable as possible.

Maeve returned quietly to Teagan's side and took the tequila bottle from her hand. Drinking deeply, licking her lips she said "mmm, I love Mexican." Her sharp teeth shining as she grinned and lit another cigarette.

"Oh me too," Teagan nodded in agreement, "anyone who could come up with something as delicious as enchilada sauce is a genius in my book." The girls laughed at one another, linking arms as they continued their journey home. Swaying slightly and singing loudly "Silver Threads among the Gold."

Maeve stayed at The Patrick's home the week leading up to her birthday and that blessed occasion was finally upon them. She had chosen a dark green dress for the evening; low cut, black ribbon tied around her trim waist and sleeves belled at the elbows. Teagan decided on deep teal colored cotton number with a scooped neckline, sleeves that hit mid bicep and a white ribbon to show off her tiny mid-section. Meagan's dress matched her sisters in design but, was opposite in color; white dress, teal ribbon.

"Anyone up for a game of Schwoozle before we head out," Meagan queried, raising a scarlet eyebrow mischievously.

"No! You always win," Matt protested.

"Fine, no Absinthe for you then. Maeve, Teagan I know you're always game."

"Excuse me ladies but, what exactly is Schwoozle," Blake asked a bit concerned.

Blake Collins had begun courting Breelan Louise a short two weeks before Maeve's birthday. The pair were already quite in love but, this was the first time her friends would meet him. She looked as lovely as ever for her dear friend's birthday party. She wore a low cut, fitted black silk dress the length of which came all the way to the floor. Her long black hair was fixed in a simple loose plait and she had rimmed her dark brown eyes with kohl. He was as dashing as Bree described him. Very tall and lean, he had wild brown hair and his blue eyes had kept their sprite hood precocity. He was very kind and gentle and absolutely in love with Bree. It was all he thought. Love.

It was very contagious. Blake had chosen to dress to fit in with the cowboys around whom they would be celebrating that night. He loved any excuse to wear his boots.

"Basically dear it is drunken croquet but, our little Meagan here loves to make up her own rules."

"Like the first player to hit a rover ball has to take a shot or, when you miss a roquet you take a shot," Teagan finished what Bree had begun.

"I'm in," Blake exclaimed exuberantly.

An hour later, with one less bottle of Absinthe in Douglas, the sextet headed to Tombstone. Maeve had decided on The Bird Cage for the night's festivities and wanted to go through the Boot hill Cemetery on the way; they all had a fascination with ghosts and the dead. Faeries believed that until one had gained all the knowledge their soul required, they continued to visit earth in physical form. Oracles were regarded as the most evolved beings and even they endured hundreds of life cycles though, theirs were by choice. Cemeteries were always interesting places because you never knew who you would encounter or, which plane of existence they may be.

Olive Glasston's copper hair whipped around her face as the ghost of a long dead cowboy swung her about over his gravestone. They heard her gleeful laughter a mile away and sped up to meet her. Olive had decided to join them for the festivities that night and Teagan couldn't have been happier about it. She was quite the wild child and a good time was sure to be had whenever she was involved. Her mother, Patricia, was an artist in New York who had gotten involved with Charles Tiffany. When she told him she was pregnant with his child his solution was to "get rid of it." Patricia Glasston decided instead to move to Arizona where no one had heard of them and she could continue doing what she loved while raising her daughter. Teagan was so very glad she did.

How fitting that Olive should arrive just now and Bree along with her, their various businesses having been shut down for the weekend she gathered, from their respective tangle of thoughts. Bree had brought along as much of the food and drink her mother had ordered as she could safely fly with, Jack and Blake would be around later with the rest and plenty of staff to take care of the cleaning up. Teagan heard the officers stationed at the west edge of her property question both Olive and Bree in turn, she heard sighs of relief from each when they'd been allowed through only to find a second and more intense round of interrogation awaited them just outside the front door. By the time they had been escorted to Galen they were ready to offer their first born children just to catch a glimpse of their friends; they were allowed to pass without such an offer and greeted their King appropriately. After being instructed to do just as Maeve had done, they got comfortable; Olive sat straight backed and cross legged. Bree followed suit, put in her ear buds and pressed play on one of she and Teagan's simultaneously discovered electro-pop songs, Olive took Maeve's free hand and Bree took Teagan's so they could begin to memory share as they had never done before.

'Excellent music choice Bree,' Maeve and Olive thought in unison.

'Thanks! It's one of Teagan's favorites.'

'Her music taste is so varied, I love it,' Olive beamed admiration.

'That it is. Music is an easy thing to get lost in when you're trying to block other people out,' Bree thought.

'Indeed. She is quite the little audiophile our Teagan,' Maeve concurred.

'It's positively weird that you can hear what I'm hearing', Bree giggled.

'Bollocks, this is mad,' Maeve thought.

'Agreed but, brilliant,' Bree thought in response.

'Why don't we do this all the time,' Olive echoed Bree's enthusiasm.

'This is what it's like to be inside Teagan's head,' they all though at once, awe and curiosity coloring their thoughts.

'Yes and she can hear you so keep it down. Now I remember why you're only allowed in one at a time,' Teagan scolded them.

'Sorry,' their chorused apology whispered across her mind.

'It's alright. At least you brought good music,' Teagan reassured them, *'since you lot are just joining us, we are in Tombstone for Maeve's birthday.'*

'Oh how fun,' Bree thought.

'Aww that's the night I met you and Blake,' Olive cooed.

'I'm glad that's where you went,' Maeve told them, *'we were just in the cemetery as Olive was dancing-'*

'Dancing with Johnny,' Olive cut Maeve off mid thought, she oozed nostalgia.

"Darlin' your eyes are the prettiest I've ever seen," the ghost of Johnny Ringo was attempting to charm the corset off Olive.

"Aren't you the sweet talker," she threw her head back and laughed heartily," thank you kindly."

"Sweet talker only in the afterlife mind you," he dropped her back for a dip, "I was as loyal a hound dog as any while I was lucky enough to be alive."

"I see," Olive grinned widely at him as she popped back up, "death hasn't robbed you of your silver tongue."

"There she is," Teagan interrupted their dance just before Olive had a chance to plant a kiss on the cowboy's cheek.

"Tis herself," Olive called back and hopped down from the top of the decrepit tombstone.

"How are you," Teagan gathered her friend to her in a tight hug.

"Very well and about to get even better," Olive answered with a wink and a smile.

"Too right you are," Teagan winked back at her, "Olive,

this is Bree and Blake, the rest of these miscreants you're familiar with already."

"Hello," Olive nodded to each in turn before embracing them briefly, "I hope you're ready to forget this lovely August night."

"We know I am," Maeve grimaced, "I am not at all keen on leaving my youth behind."

"Be glad you've lived to experience it darlin'," Johnny told her from his perch on his gravestone, "and give Morgan my regards, will you?"

"Of course I will. To the first and the second," Maeve called over her shoulder as they made their way down the hill to one of her favorite towns to celebrate her coming of age.

Tombstone in 1919 was not the booming silver mining town it had been in 1877 nor was it the rough Earp sheriffed municipality it had become during 1882; still it was just as bustling and depraved as ever and greeted the troupe of Folk with booze fueled enthusiasm.

"Olive darlin' we could you use a hand over here," the bar tender called to her over the din as soon as he'd spotted her coming in the door.

"Be right there Jonah," Olive called back and nodded momentary leave to her friends before she picked her way through the crowd, waving off whistles and cat calls as she went. Saloons were a necessary evil as far as Olive was concerned. She was increasingly disappointed in her fellow man every shift she worked but, it paid a decent wage and most of them tipped her well because of the way she looked. She jumped up onto the bar and slid back behind it in one motion. She started taking orders while Teagan and the rest were picking out a table that wasn't too crowded, Teagan and Blake hung back to survey the room for any serious danger.

"She is one of my best friends you know," she said to him out of the side of her mouth as she scanned the left side of the room meticulously.

"I know," he responded in kind while scanning the right side.

"You know I will hurt you if you hurt her then?"

"I do but, do you really feel it is necessary to threaten me?"

"No," she said catching his eye, "I don't but, it still needed to be said."

"Fair enough," he inclined his cowboy hat her direction, "I do love her so."

"I know," Teagan nodded acceptance.

"So, how exactly does your ability work?"

"It's a bit soon for that," she said wryly, "that kind of information requires more than your admission of love for my friend, friend."

"Very well, I hope you trust me enough to share some day," he smiled down at her.

"Here you are dears," Bree stood between them after handing each a glass of water, "I'm glad we have you two staying sober tonight."

"Tombstone requires it," Teagan responded after a mouthful of warm water had slaked her parched throat.

"It surely does," Bree agreed, "where is Morgan?"

"Did someone request the presence of an orphaned child of a man who tamed this town," Morgan Earp's mischievous grin had appeared at Teagan's right shoulder just as her name was mentioned. The human daughter of Louisa Houstin and

Morgan Earp had been raised by her mother's relations after her widowed mother died giving birth to her. She ran away to Tombstone when she was sixteen and started working as a bar back at The Bloody Bucket where she quickly earned a reputation as a pragmatic and scrupulous businesswoman; word had also spread like wildfire that she had a wicked right hook and was an excellent shot. The now thirty-seven-year-old newly minted Madame of The Black Canary pulled out all the stops for Maeve's birthday it seemed; her dark blonde hair was expertly curled and pinned beneath her smart black top hat, the peacock blue of her silk gown was carried beautifully by her desert sun tanned skin and her brown eyes were framed by liner and lashes of the finest make. She was Teagan's height but had Bree's petite build and her corset was certainly doing a fine job creating as much cleavage as possible with what little it had to work with.

"Ah and how is my favorite lady of the night," Teagan greeted her with a hug and kiss on the cheek.

"Business is good," she beamed, "ladies always pay better than men do though, and I don't have to keep them in line as violently."

"I would assume as much," Blake said with a raised brow.

"Hello there, I'm Morgan," she reached out a freshly ungloved hand to shake his.

"Hello Morgan, I'm Blake."

"Charmed I'm sure," turning to Bree she asked, "is this one yours then? He is very handsome."

"Yes, I just happen to be so lucky," Bree smiled widely and hugged Blake sideways.

"Indeed. Where is our little Fuil Leannan then? I have missed her so these past months."

"I believe that is her on the bar with Olive," Teagan raised her water glass in their direction.

"Oh my, that does look scrumptious," Morgan licked her lips and made haste to her lover.

"Oi! Bree get over here for a shot," Meagan yelled from atop the bar stool she had just slid down onto after Olive poured whiskey from the bottle straight into her mouth.

"Not if I have to take it like that," Bree called as she cut through the crowd to the group at the bar.

"Oh come on now where is your sense of adventure," Olive shook the half full bottle at her as she pulled her next customer over to do the same, the lucky cowboy gladly tipped his hat to Olive when she scooped it off his head, put it on her own and pulled his hair back to pour liquor down his throat. She sealed it with a kiss and placed his hat back on his head when she was finished, he placed a significant amount of paper money into her cleavage before stumbling over his boots back to his table.

"Who's next then eh," Jonah the bar tender asked the crowd, "form an orderly queue gents!"

Morgan had finally found Maeve at the table their party had commandeered and was guiding the already inebriated Faerie to a room above the saloon; their show was met with applause and whistles aplenty, to which the pair only giggled and rolled their eyes. Ever the show-woman, Morgan pulled Maeve to her in a deep and passionate kiss just in front of their door before they entered to share each other as is still forbidden in many parts of the world. This display was met with silence and wide-open gobs before a few encouraging whoops were heard throughout the room. Teagan too just rolled her eyes and settled back into keeping watch from her post near the exit, Blake had gone to get them fresh water and a snack.

Teagan was eyeing a man that had been sidling closer to Matt since he had taken up the bench at the poker table; he was of average height, build, appearance and very friendly. Too average. Too friendly. Keeping her guard up, she focused her energy on pushing into his mind. She immediately regretted the decision; he was a Kelpie called Donovan who had been blacklisted from every brothel within fifty miles for the abuse he had inflicted on women. His appearance was a facade, not a strong one but it did well enough to fool the drunk and only getting drunker patrons. He was after Morgan for being the proponent of such an action and was only waiting for his opportunity to rip out her throat. When he turned this way or that, Teagan made out his squelching, dark horse appearance.

Teagan recoiled from his thoughts just as Blake was returning with their provisions and she was glad of his timing.

"See that man over there," Teagan whispered when she took her glass and nodded in Donovan's direction.

"Yes," Blake responded also barely above a whisper, "something is not right about him."

"Correct, I need you to start a fight with him," Teagan instructed.

"What," Blake nearly choked on his water.

"Act drunk and bump into him," she suggested, "he is so highly strung he will overreact so be careful."

"You're serious."

"As a rattle snake bite."

"You'll fill me in later?"

"You have my word," she promised and drained the last of her water, "I'm going to apprise Olive of what's to happen. Don't stumble over to him until you see me climbing the railing to the second floor. Matt will join in the fray whether we like it or not, make sure Meagan is out of the way, I'll take care of Bree."

"Yes ma'am," he nodded acknowledgement and pursed his lips, preparing for a scuffle.

Nervous that her last-minute plan would fall apart, she swallowed her fear and swayed her way to Olive at the bar; not that anyone was really paying attention at this point but, should Donovan happen to be watching her she wanted to make sure she appeared properly intoxicated. She slammed her glass down in front of Olive and pulled herself nearly back behind the bar to get her attention. Sitting side saddle on the wet with spilled alcohol wood, she pulled Olive's face close enough to her own that it looked like they were kissing.

"See that man by Matt," she whispered into Olive's ear amongst the hooting and hollering the degenerate male patrons were providing.

"The Kelpie with the poor glamour?"

"Yes, he is here to kill Morgan we need to get everyone out safely," she pushed back a bit and blushed before leaning into Olive's other ear, "do you have your pistol ready?"

"Always prepared for a fight my love," she responded by pulling Teagan's hair back a bit and leaning into her neck, "what's the plan?"

"Blake is going to start a fight with him," Teagan replied barely above a whisper, eyes closed in faux pleasure, "Matt will join in surely. I need you to get Meagan and Bree down behind the bar."

"I'm on it," she pushed Teagan's face back up to meet her own, inciting another round of loud cheers, "our Sapphic sisters upstairs?"

"I'm on it," Teagan kissed her quickly on the mouth and winked as she stood to pull herself up the railing to the second floor. Checking behind her briefly, she saw Blake moving into position and burst through the door where her friends had unfortunately only just begun in earnest.

"I'm so sorry to interrupt ladies but, hold that thought and put your clothes back on," she announced after slamming the door securely shut behind her.

"Teagan what is the meaning of this," Maeve protested pulling the sheets up to cover herself.

"Come now darling the more the merrier," Morgan suggested from her position at Maeve's waist.

"I'm flattered really but, not my choice of fare and we need to get you both out of here," she had to shout above the loud bang and subsequent shouting that had announced Olive's pistol being used downstairs.

"Turn around then and explain while we are dressing," Maeve requested.

"Make it quick please," Teagan said over her shoulder, "there is a Kelpie downstairs who is bent on killing your missus."

"That fucker Donovan," Morgan huffed, hastily pulling up her bloomers.

"That'd be the one," Teagan nodded.

"Why does he want to kill you darling," Maeve inquired, hastening into her dress.

"I've had him blacklisted for being a woman beater," she responded hurriedly, there was another loud bang and the three heard shuffling at the bottom of the stairs.

"That's it! Get to that window now," Teagan yelled and turned to grab the chair that was sitting at the vanity, she wedged it under the doorknob to buy them a few extra seconds. Donovan, glamour abandoned and part way back to his true form, turned the wood to splinters with a swift kick of his hoof with Teagan the only faerie left in the room, he stomped over to the window as fast as his horse legs would carry him and jumped out after her. Hovering in wait just above the open window, she snatched him by his slippery mane as he shot out like a cannon ball after her and her friends, ignoring his screeches of pain she threw him to the hard ground below and stayed just out of reach of his still human hands. Maeve had taken Morgan around to the front to fetch the others.

"So, you think it's fun to abuse women do you," she menaced, hovering inches from his face.

"Fun isn't the word I would use," he swiped fruitlessly at Teagan with a heavy fist.

"Oh? What word would you use then," she teased, licking his chin.

"Satisfying," he grinned evilly as she zipped back again just out of reach.

"You'll forgive me being satisfied at what your about to

endure then won't you," she pinned him down at the wrists and hooves just as her friends were rounding the corner.

"Teagan," Meagan cried out, Matt held his struggling beloved back with little effort.

"Stay back you lot," Teagan called without breaking eye contact with the Kelpie's penetrating gaze, "this one here is about to get what he deserves."

Taking a deep breath, she dug into his twisted mind and bent it to her will, warping his thoughts to believe he was a cat; Kelpies live and breathe in water, cats avoid it at all cost and while it may not have been the most creative solution it was the best she could come up with just then, without expending too much energy on the wretch. He was more resistant than Teagan had anticipated but, it took less than a minute to empty his waterlogged brain and fill it with feline proclivities. She released her hold and he just lay there for a moment staring blankly up at them all. After what seemed like ages, he rolled over on all fours and mewed pathetically, striding awkwardly over to Morgan and rubbing himself against her legs. She shewed him away roughly and he ran from her as fast as his ungainly gait would allow. They all rounded on Teagan who was laughing heartily at her cleverness and Maeve cleared her throat in lieu of questioning her friend.

"So, Donovan now believes he is a cat," she barely got out between giggles.

"He what," a disbelieving Blake asked hesitantly.

"He believes he is a cat," Teagan repeated, wiping tears from the corners of her eyes.

"Seriously," Maeve could not hide her grin.

"Seriously," a breathless Teagan responded, now shaking with laughter, and guiding herself gently to the ground.

"Holy hell," Morgan shook her head and began chuckling.

"Remind me never to make you angry," Blake said before allowing himself a laugh as well.

Between the drink, their adrenaline and Donovan the cat, soon they were all rolling in the dirt or wiping tears from their cheeks amidst their fits of laughter.

As soon as their memory sharing had finished, Olive, Maeve and Bree got up as slowly as possible to avoid moving too suddenly. Teagan had come back to the present with them and was sleeping soundly but, would soon be handed over to her mother for an overdue bath and some coddling. The trio of her oldest friends made their way to the kitchen to help the Collin's Pub and Jack's Bistro staff, their respective proprietors included, set out the fare the Patrick matriarch had ordered. There would be no party but, those close to the McCarthy and Patrick families would be arriving soon to offer help in any way that was required of them and to hold each other up should the worst happen; there would be plenty of bellies to fill and the Queen didn't want anything to go to waste. The older generation had endured The Second Fae War and knew all too well that things could go sour just as easily as it may go in their favor and in less than a blink of an eye either direction. Blake set down the tureen he was wiping out with a clean dry cloth and hugged his wife to him as tears began to fall down her cheeks. Jack gathered Maeve and Olive to him in similar fashion as they each spilled their tears onto his shoulders.

"It'll be alright dears," Blake patted Bree's back and said to the room in hopes of comforting them all.

"How are they," Jack asked uncertainly.

"They are still here for the moment," Timothy answered as he entered the kitchen.

"What about the baby," the ladies asked at once.

"Doctor Monaghan will be here soon to give her a once over but, from what I can gather he is fine."

"It's a boy," Olive's excitement subdued but, only just.

"Aye, it's a boy," King Patrick smiled sadly, heading for the fridge, "they're tough, they'll be alright."

"True," Jack nodded, "and if Rylan dies Teagan will kill him."

"That she will," the King chuckled softly, "now, where is this cherry cider my wife ordered? It's a two-drink minimum kind of night."

Brick

When Airioch's tossing and turning in the space she'd taken up between she and Rylan woke her, Teagan lay clinging to her better half on their bed; it was as much as she'd allowed herself to be moved since they crash landed at the edge of their property. She felt like one big bruise, even the air in her lungs ached. She wasn't sure what day it was, how long it had been since she shut everyone out and couldn't quite remember who had come and gone. Everything was blending together, faces, voices, smells. They were all just out of reach it seemed; like a terrible nightmare where she was once again Teagan the Mute. Someone, her mother maybe, had scrubbed her clean and changed her clothes. Galen had come in and done the same for Rylan. She remembered that. She remembered it because he had not spoken to or attempted to speak with her. He had actively thought of nothing aside from exactly what he was there to do. He was disappointed in her, that much he could not hide. She was disappointed too but could not force herself back into her daily life. Not without Rylan. She felt as though leaving him there, comatose as he was, was a betrayal.

She feared he wouldn't wake up or, maybe he would die

and if he died while she wasn't there, she would never forgive herself letting him die alone. She felt like a sprite trying to avoid chores on the weekend; if she hit the snooze button when it sounded every five minutes and hit it hard enough perhaps the day would be delayed altogether. 'Just five more minutes' she thought. Just five more minutes and she could hit Rylan's 'play' button. She could bring him back. She could save him if she stayed. 'Time' she thought. She needed more time. Of the myriad things her ability provided, like the memory sharing she remembered having with her friends at some point while she was unconscious, time was not really one of them. She could not change it, reverse its consequences or give more of it. She had to stay with him, had to find the pause button and release it.

She fell back into their cocoon. Blocked out the reality of the present and let the physical world fall away. They were naked in the dark, sitting in Lotus as if finishing a yoga session beneath the willow in their private backyard sanctuary. She watched him breathe deeply in and exhale just as powerfully. Eyes closed, the backs of his hands rested on the top of his crossed knees, the pads of his thumb and forefinger on each hand touching each other.

Only light emanated from their bodies, their auras, Rylan's was a pale purple and white. All she could get from him now was 'family.' That's what he was stuck on. He had been frightened and thrust himself head long into the fray to save those he loved, ever the infantry man her Rylan Robert McCarthy.

For the second time in his life, he truly feared he would lose everything. This was not good. White meant death or, near to it. Rylan was usually beautiful shades of turquoise, yellow and green; content, in control and happy to lead the way through any situation. She looked down at herself and concern set in immediately. Where she was usually a lovely blend of electric blue and brilliant orange now, she was dirty grey and ugly sulfur.

Except her belly where their child was actively growing; a stunning hot pink surrounded by turquoise and purple. Her son, *their* son, was happy. Exuding love, spirituality and understanding energy from inside his safe haven. She cradled her pregnant core, which was substantially fuller here than in their physical plane and looked up at her husband. He was static, his thoughts, position and breath unchanged. What she was about to do was wrong and she knew it. It was a betrayal of their trust and would break a promise she never dreamed of breaking. Before going back and letting him heal or pass on she had to know one thing for certain and for that she would need to mess about in his brain. When Rylan left the IRA for the REF, he ceased contact with her. Intermittently throughout their marriage she had insisted he had done so because he had fallen out of love with her. She was sure that he had grown tired of her worrying and of waiting to come home to her. She was sure that he wanted to go back to his Fae-Whoring ways while he was stationed abroad.

She was no fool, she had heard the stories; French ladies cared not that the men for whom they opened their legs had sweethearts back home. He always told her she was wrong, that he had shut her out to protect her. He had closed himself off because he did not want her exposed to the horrors of war. He never got angry with her when her old insecurity crept in, he just smiled sadly and kissed her hands.

"Rylan forgive me," she said before breaching the boundaries of his mind and taking them back to a time before war had changed them, six years before they'd become husband and wife...

"Well, you'll be back in Douglas with your family, and I thought it would be a good way to pass the time between our visits," Rylan explained his extreme and rash decision to join the Irish Republican Brotherhood as they strolled hand in hand down the long dirt road leading back to his family home, The spring mist cooling the air around them just enough.

"Let me get this straight. You're in a long-distance relationship with 'the girl of your dreams', your words not mine, and volunteering for The Brotherhood is the best way to pass the time between," Teagan asked, frustration coming out on her tongue. She let go of Rylan's hand and unnecessarily adjusted the white cotton skirts of her summer dress, folding her hands behind her back when she was finished. Exasperated, Rylan tucked his own hands in the pockets of his grey tweed trousers.

"Our fathers were United and our grandfathers before them," he stubbornly retorted more forcefully than he had intended.

"Oh so, it's a Fenian you are now? Shall I start calling you Teague and sing 'Poor Paddy on the Railway' every time you enter the room," she fired back, her frustration flushing her cheeks.

"They were soldiers is all I meant," he said more evenly,

not wishing to push her temper further than he was prepared to deal with.

"Yes, in *FAE* wars that were thrust upon them. They were not United Irishmen longer than their common sense would allow," her cheeks still a darker shade of pink than Rylan would have liked.

"Bah! Human? Fae? What does it matter? War affects us all," his own temper raising his voice from his throat and his hands from his pockets.

"Human war affects Fae when humans are taken for pawns in UnSeelie games. This is not the case! Religion has torn apart greater countries than Ireland Rylan Robert. De Valera is nothing more than a rabble rouser and mark my words, he'll turn on his friend Michael quicker than you can say "Free State," she had let her anger consume her and had shouted the last at Rylan as she hastened away from him. Hands balled into fists around the skirts she had hiked to her knees, her narrowed gaze was on the path ahead of her, cheeks as red as the hair pulling free of its loose bun at the nape of her neck from the effort of her frenzied pace. Rylan had nearly been run over when cut directly in front of her, he may not have had wings but, he still possessed Fae athleticism.

"Move," she demanded through clenched teeth.

"I will not," his Irish Brogue never thicker than, when he was trying to be more charming than he actually was.

She unclenched her fists and crossed her arms in front of her. He reached out his hands and placed one on either elbow in an attempt to pull her to him. When she would not budge, he moved closer to her and wrapped his arms around her shoulders, closing his eyes and letting his cheek rest on top of her head.

"The Irish deserve their freedom, as do all beings. That is why I want to join. I believe in this," he said quietly.

"I don't," his stubborn lover protested, "What about all that Iron and poisonous fume? Did you think about that?"

"There are masks and suits to prevent me harm."

"Those are not meant to be worn more than a week at a time and even that is a stretch," she argued, her temper slowly changing to the worry it stemmed from.

"Then I'll just have to take my own stockpile won't I," he moved back just enough to lift her chin with his left index finger, looking down into her green eyes, still bright with fury.

"You really believe in this? You aren't just trying to be a hero," she inquired her anger all but, gone.

"Oh, I don't know, maybe hero looks good on me. Besides, I hear ladies love scars," he winked at her and smiled broadly.

"You know what ladies don't love? Their men in pine boxes," she narrowed her eyes at him. Their fight was over but she wanted to make sure he understood she was worried.

"We both know I've never looked good in pine. Birch is really more fashionable this season anyways," he brushed her cheekbone softly with the back of his left hand.

"Come home safely to me or, not at all."

"Aye ma'am," he said into her mouth before he kissed her.

She helped him collect and pack all the things he would need, including plenty of "Second Skin" Faerie hazmat suits and stationary to write to her if the mood struck, it never would. She put him on the train to Belfast with a parting kiss and threat to kill him if he died. It would be six years before she saw his smile again. The memory she was in, bled into another she had plucked from his thoughts, the betrayal she was there for, the memory that would either assuage her ego or crush it forever.

France in the spring of 1918 was cold, wet, and dreary. It was miserable and reminded him of home but lacked Ireland's charm. What he wouldn't give to be half drunk at Molly Bloom's making wives mad at the money their husbands were losing to him at poker.

At least there the only projectiles aimed at him were pint glasses and slurred insults. Arras during wartime was not Easter 1916. It was hell. Three years ago, he thought bombs were fun and relished the thrill of hunting Protestant Irish traitors, having seen his friends blown apart before him had changed his mind. Having the blood of twenty-year-old men spattered on your face will do that. Holding your bunk mates rib cage together as the light leaves his eyes will do that. Having your Sergeants bloody handprint left on your camouflage after he dies in your arms, sobbing that he would never meet his son, will do that.

He squinted hard to see through the blear in his eyes and the pain in his bones from poison seeping through his many layers. He had been wearing the same Second Skin and same uniform for two weeks now and even the trudge back to base was like sand grating against sunburnt skin.

His muscles burned from the effort of pulling his boots from the mud that threatened to suck his soul down into it, his breath labored from the effort of trying to filter out what his failing protective gear could not. All his energy was bent on moving his body forward, he was grateful Teagan wasn't in his head anymore. This is not a version of himself he would have her know. It was a version of himself whose boots she'd tie and ass she'd kick for not taking care of the man to whom they belonged. It was a version of himself she'd not recognize, lose sleep over or look twice at. Rylan was sure of one thing, war is hell. Ugly, cruel hell. He meant to get out alive and hoped he could do so before the devil knew he was there.

Somewhere in the time it took for his brain to send the message to his eyelids to blink but, before he could execute his body's request, the muscles in his legs gave way and he fell to his knees in the muddy sea that threatened to consume him. His hands went slack and his rifle fell in front of him along with what was left of his will to trudge. The message having finally been received, he closed his eyes, breathed deeply and let himself fall backward; his torso hit the ground with an eerie squelch and his rucksack dug awkwardly into his back. His helmet slid off his head and into the most uncomfortable pillow he had ever known but, he no longer cared. He had nothing left. He just wanted to sleep. Five minutes, just five bloody minutes of respite.

"McCarthy," he heard the familiar voice shout before the sound of hastily moving boots and rattling mess kit had reached his ears.

"I'm up," he winced.

"Rylan we can't stop," Galen Murphy had finally reached him.

"I know. I just need to rest," Rylan plead through cracked lips.

"Not yet brother. Almost. Get up, come on," Galen nudged

him with the butt of his own rifle, saved from the muddy tempest that nearly devoured it.

"I can't," he exhaled painfully.

"Yes, you can. You will, you must," Galen insisted.

"I am nothing Len. My soul aches and threatens to forsake me," he lamented.

"Come now don't be dramatic. You know ladies aren't allowed to play war and more evil men than you still have their souls. Get up," he rattled him with the heel of his boot.

"No. Just leave me here."

"No," Galen kicked his right hip.

"Fuck, that hurts," Rylan protested.

"Keep laying here mate and you'll not be feeling anything ever again."

"Good."

"No. Get. Up," Galen dug the toe of his boot under Rylan's right hip and lifted.

"Stop pestering me! I just want a nap!"

Just then, the sky let loose all the rain it had only previously been misting on them. As though this downpour were the signal for more mayhem, they heard a fresh round of mortar fire sounding closer than their already uncomfortable selves would have liked.

"You'll get a permanent one soon enough if you don't move."

"Galen, please."

"No," he landed another kick, harder this time.

"Fuck you."

"No, fuck you. I'm not leaving you here to fertilize French

soil and I'll not get killed because you fancy a nap," he kicked him again.

"Stop it asshole."

"What would Teagan do," Galen goaded him from his position now kneeling at Rylan's side. The latter's eyes snapped open and immediately narrowed at the former.

"You keep her name out of your mouth."

"Ah that has your attention now. Good. Get up," the only man blonder than Rylan McCarthy himself pulled his weary comrade back up to a kneeling position.

"I'm so tired Len."

"I know. A scrub and a meal will help. We must move though," he pulled them to their feet as another round of thunder and mortar fire crashed even closer than the first.

"I don't think my legs will work."

"They will. Come on, one foot in front of the other," he pushed Rylan's right foot forward with his own.

"She must never know of this," Rylan implored him, tears welling up in his eyes.

"Who must never know of what," Galen handed Rylan his rifle and patted him on the back as they set back to base as fast as their weary legs would carry them.

Teagan came to, tasting the salt from her own tears on her lips. At the end of the bed Galen Murphy knelt muttering to himself, holding a foot of either McCarthy in each of his hands.

"Please, you must wake. We have survived too much for you to leave me now brother. You saved him before, you must do it again. He would not want you to perish on his account. Teagan, what he wouldn't do for you..."

"He would pull me from the mud," she whispered, sitting up and crawling to Galen at the foot of the bed. He did not hide the shock on his face or, the tears streaming down it when she gathered him to her in a reassuring hug.

"Aye he would. Pull him from the mud Princess. Save him as only you know how. We need you both," his tears spilled onto her night shirt as he plead into her shoulder.

"Aye sir. I will do the best I can," she said quietly into his unwashed hair before kissing his forehead and rocking them silently.

She looked to her right where Rylan's chair sat next to their bed, Josephine had been placed there next to a copy of one of Teagan's favorite records and a pack of chocolate Necco wafers. Her family had never left her side, she let her emotion consume her and cried along with her husband's best friend, rocking them both long into the morning.

BURN

Burn

After two and a half months of sitting idly at home with her family, another two stuck behind her desk and enduring countless hours with the department psychiatrist, the now visibly pregnant Teagan was relieved to be back at work and put to use. The Soul Reaver Augustana Von Dotch sat stiff backed with ankles crossed in the intentionally uncomfortable wooden chair in the interrogation room. Eyes closed, hands folded on the table in front of her, her youthful visage did not reflect the creatures more than 600 years spent on the planet thus far. Her pale blonde hair was teased, tied up and hair sprayed into a perfect faux hawk, her equally pale eyebrows groomed expertly, her naturally translucent and unfairly long eyelashes mascaraed to a midnight black today; a glittery red gloss slicked across her thin pout and pale pink blush brushed across her high cheek bones to help her alabaster skin look human was the only other makeup she wore. Her small chest was unmoving under the thin fabric of her white V-neck t-shirt. Her long, slim legs carried the black skinny jeans that covered them as well as any model would have, and her purple glitter peep toe pumps gave her an additional five inches of height that made her taller than most male's when she stood up.

If Teagan wasn't any the wiser, Augustana could easily have passed for a singer in a punk rock band. Detective McCarthy smoothed her black, short sleeved tunic length shirt down over her leggings when she sat down in the chair across from the Vampire already seated at the table and actively tried to avoid touching her belly. She was always touching her belly these days. It was as though she could hold her son in the palm of her hand, she felt closer to him that way. She felt closer to Rylan that way; Rylan who was still in suspended animation. She set down the blue folder she had brought into the room with her and set it on the table. Opening it to the place she needed, she removed the pen she had tucked into the binding and folded her hands on her lap in front of her. The Vampire did not move or, acknowledge the Faeries presence in any way.

Vampire was a broad and somewhat incorrect term. Augustana was a Soul Reaver, one of the last of her kind and from what Teagan knew she was the gentlest as well. Soul Reaver's did not take the blood of their prey but, their essence; their souls and their memories. Once a Reaver had your soul they had you forever and could make use of your memories at any time. It was what they thrived on; other creature's energy and experiences. Teagan was extra careful to block her own mind; her ability controlled by a Reaver would be lethal. If said Reaver was particularly depraved, they could end her people altogether. That was not something Teagan would be responsible for, she shivered at the thought. The being in front of her had some knowledge about who was responsible for the attack on her and her husband. It was time to put her skills back to work.

"Augustana Von Dotch, do you know why you are here," Teagan began.

"I can only assume it has to do with your husband," her voice was high but, raspy and she sounded like she hailed from Eastern Europe, though where exactly, Teagan could not place.

"What makes you think I have a husband?"

"I am six times your age. I have consumed more life than you will ever bear. Show some respect," she spoke barely above a whisper and kept her eyes closed as she answered, "You're pregnant, at least six months along I would guess and Fae generally do not breed without being partnered. I know you and your husband were attacked. Four months ago wasn't it?"

"That is correct," Teagan responded staring at the eyelids of her suspect.

"I am sorry for that but, I had no part in it."

"Thank you but, that is not why you are here."

"Isn't it? Do get on with it then. We haven't much time Faerie."

"You were an elf before being turned weren't you?"

"I was."

"I don't know much about Reaver's. How does one end up being what you are?"

"It's a history lesson I was brought for then? Can I at least get a beverage?"

"Certainly. What would you like?

"Shirley Temple, iced, extra cherries with two shots of vodka."

"Very well," Teagan nodded and one of the officers observing behind the bullet-proof two-way mirror went to fetch Augustana's drink.

"Done. Now, where were you?"

"There weren't always so few of us," she began her voice still barely above a whisper; eyelids closed, "During the Great Fae War of 1346 The UnSeelie Queen, Anise, unbeknownst to her King had convinced a Warlock with whom she had been consorting to teach her his dark magic. She wanted to create an army of Elves who could survive off of the energy of the living instead of food or, water. She was certain that consuming another's soul would make one all powerful and increase the already superhuman strength innate to the Elven race."

Officer Jones entered the room as she finished her opening statements and placed her requested thirst quencher in front of her. His tall blonde self, stood over her a bit longer than was necessary before exiting and shutting the door behind him harder than he should have, a move which garnered naught but an annoyed glare from Augustana.

"Ego never ceases to amaze me," she huffed leaning forward to take a sip from her glass.

"Nor me and I have to work with an unfair amount of it," Teagan chuckled.

"You chose this profession Faerie, I'm surprised your own ego isn't over inflated."

"Not really my thing. I chose Public Safety because I am good at helping others and I enjoy civil service; even if we aren't always so civil."

"I'm not so sure you understand incivility, the tactics your kind use are far less brutal than many I've seen and endured in my long life," she smiled sadly and gulped another mouthful of her 'Dirty Shirley.' Speaking as they were, Augustana seemed leagues away from the lethal creature Teagan knew her to be and she could easily see how one could be charmed into trusting her.

"Indeed. Now, what about The Queen and The Great Fae War," Teagan pressed.

"After he taught her the magic required, Anise convinced her lover to be her first sacrifice, convinced him he would lead her army of dark elves; He was merely a shining example of loves blindness. She took his soul, bound it to her own, and killed him before his last breath left his lungs. She was the very first Soul Reaver and the mother of us all," she coughed out the last word and breathed deeply to steady herself.

"It was your brother wasn't it? The one who turned you?"

"Yes," she answered, Grey eyes flashing menacingly, "He was not himself. He was mad with grief and pain. All did not go as Anise had planned. She unwisely chose her former lovers for minions and sacrificed her own children to do so. When her husband, King Braeltos, realized what she had done he passed his crown to their oldest son and killed himself before their subjects. Prince Riven would become the most even-tempered King in the UnSeelie court; he also had the shortest reign. The Queen fled the kingdom and wandered the Southern Woods with her Harem, preying on innocent travelers and wayward rangers. My brother was one such innocent. He had just proposed to and been rejected by Brynn Patrick;

your aunt and Princess of the Sulann. He let his heartbreak decide his fate and mine."

"I've never heard this story. How can I be sure it's true?"

"You've heard your father tell you stories about your grandfather being a Reaver Slayer?"

"Yes," Teagan answered slowly.

"He killed Anise. He let me watch."

"Did he now," the guilt knotted at Teagan's throat dissipated somewhat.

"He did. I wanted to kill her but, he could not justify letting a 'child' lose her soul," she laughed at the irony of his chivalry.

"He let you live, he could have ended your life as well."

"No, he couldn't have. He saw me as a child and could not move to strike. *I* let *him* live, you're welcome," she nearly growled at her interrogator before another cough escaped her throat. When she removed the hand that covered her mouth, an ink blue substance clung to the corners of her lips.

"Are you dying Augustana?"

"I told you we hadn't much time," Grey eyes glared at Teagan through long lashes.

"Jones, notify Siobhan we will be needing her services soon," Teagan said over her shoulder.

"Calling the Banshee already? I'm not even cold yet! Well, I am but, not ready to be buried," Augustana jested.

"I thought Reaver's lived forever?"

"Slow acting poison. Copper and nutmeg injected intravenously."

"Who sent you," Teagan asserted, trying to keep her sudden panic from her voice.

"No one. I came of my own accord. He knew I would."

"Who did?"

"Please ask me what you need to ask."

Teagan pulled a picture of the victim from the Collins murder out of her file folder and slid it across the table for Augustana to study.

"That man was killed in a Public House nearly five months ago. You were speaking with him when it happened."

"Five months ago? No, no I have not seen that man for at least one hundred years."

'*I know you can hear me Princess,*' the Reaver's voice whispered into her mind, '*the answers you seek cannot be spoken aloud.*'

'*You are protected here,*' Teagan assured her.

"Look again. There is no rush."

'*It isn't me I'm trying to protect.*'

"No, I am certain I have not seen him for at least a century and certainly not in the Pub you're speaking about."

'*Very well, We'll have to put on a good show though.*'

'*Agreed,*' Augustana raised a pale brow mischievously.

"Come now soul sucker, do you really want the last thing you say in your wretched life to be a fucking lie?"

Augustana was across the table, right hand tightening around Teagan's throat before the last word fell from her lips.

"What did I tell you about being respectful Faerie," she whispered into Teagan's left ear as the officers watching behind the glass scrambled to get into the room, "I am hungry. You and your child would be delicious."

She ran the tip of her purple tongue along the edge of Teagan's pointed ear and released her just as half a squad of patrol officers exploded into the room, prepared for a fight. The Sergeant bound The Reaver Von Dotch to her chair with iron handcuffs secured behind her back.

"I'm fine Jake," Teagan insisted when he had checked her over like a mother dog, "have Jones bring her a straw as she has decided she can no longer behave herself."

Augustana coughed another mouthful of blood and spat it in Teagan's face, grinning psychotically, her teeth now nearly black with blood.

"That's twice now you've assaulted an officer," she said, acting revolted as she wiped the sick from her cheek.

"And?"

'Good job. Anyone spying on us will never believe you'd give anything up.'

'Good. You must tell no one of this. I need your word Detective.'

'You have my word,' Teagan nodded almost imperceptibly.

"And I'd end you now if you were not already dying before me," she responded aggressively, raising her voice nearly to a yell.

"Please don't flex your wings because I bruised your little ego. You need something from me or, I wouldn't be here."

"Fair enough, let's start over then, shall we? Augustana Von Dotch you are being detained on suspicion of the murders of Orion Red Birch and Blair Phillips. I'll ask you again, how do you know this man?"

'For the sake of starting over; I was born Velika Abramovich not Augustana Von Dotch. The man you are looking for was called Blair Phillips while he was alive. The UnSeelie Queen calls him Kaius.'

Augustana, or, Velika as she was born, leaned forward to take a long pull from her now half full glass of alcohol. She stifled a wince as the cool liquid rushed down her rapidly desiccating throat, an angry looking bruise blooming at her sternum.

"He had a death wish that one. He had fallen on hard times financially and wanted to end his life. He was handsome, I was bored and hungry. He was murdered before I had the chance to oblige him."

'Orion?'

'Collateral damage. The Queen couldn't have him telling you the truth. Same reason he poisoned me.'

"Do you know the mercenary who murdered him?"

'Orion poisoned you?'

'He did it to spare me. He did not want her taking revenge.'

'That sounds like him. Who interrupted you?'

"Who doesn't know of him? He works for the King sometimes, does his dirty work. No one ever knows where or when he'll be."

'I followed the healers to hospital. When they couldn't save him, they left him to die. I tried to draw out his soul but, couldn't.'

'What prevented your necromancy?'

"Which King Reaver? You know my kind have many."

'Remember your promise. You must keep what I tell you to yourself. You gave your word.'

"The Winter King," Velika confirmed what Teagan knew she would say; further proving her innocence as the detective was aware there was no Winter King.

'I remember. You have my word.'

"And what do you mean 'when' he'll be?"

"Andreaus is a time traveler. He is everywhere and nowhere, any time, all the time."

The porcelain skin on her chest was now dark blue, the blood seeping through and staining her shirt. Her breathing began to sound more like a freight train carrying a heavy load and less like the gentle voice it usually carried. The delicate skin under her large dark eyes began to sink into the sockets; she bit her lower lip to keep blood from spraying when she coughed.

"The Winter King is dead."

'Who interrupted you Reaver?'

"He is now thanks to his wife but, then he was very much alive."

'Tylane is coming for you. Kaius is her weapon. Your sister Tyffani ruined what I tried to finish that night; his soul was nearly gone; she should have let him pass.'

One last breath railed through her lungs, she closed her eyes as she fell forward, her shoulders pulled from their sockets as the cuffs held her wrists where they were; her skull cracked when it hit the tabletop. Blood trickled from her open mouth onto the picture of a man she had once thought of as breakfast.

Cherries and ice scattered across the table; the maraschino red a stark contrast to the navy blue that once ran through her veins. Velika Abramovich was born an Elf Princess of the Novgorod Republic during the winter of 1328; she died handcuffed to a chair in a Faerie Law Enforcement station interrogation room, in 2006. She was 678 years old, the gentlest creature ever to be called Reaver and Teagan McCarthy owed her her life, she would never forget it. A sharp rap on the door pulled Teagan from the myriad thoughts racing across her mind.

"Yes?"

"Siobhan is here Detective. Can we let her in, she's freaking people out," Smith advised her anxiously.

"Yes, send her in," she instructed smoothing her dress unnecessarily when she stood up.

A tall woman wearing a black cloak entered the room, purple hair braided and just visible beneath her hood.

"Ah Siobhan! Delightfully creepy to see you as always," Teagan said brightly.

"As always, glad it's not your soul I'm guiding home today. Seeing as I didn't bring the family coach, we wouldn't have enough room for all of you anyway," the Banshee replied through the black cloth mask covering the lower half of her face.

"We're both glad of that."

"Aye princess," Siobhan winked at Teagan.

"Will you have a moment to chat after you clear up?"

"As long as nothing else comes up in my zone, there shouldn't be a problem. You know we don't take reservations, yes?"

"Yes, thank you," she laughed and shook her head, "I'll leave you to it then."

A short half hour later, Siobhan entered Teagan's office after her soft knock at the door had been acknowledged; removing her mask and gloves she took the seat across from Teagan at her desk. Banshees are strikingly beautiful aside from their mouths; thus, the masks they wore covering from just under their perfect noses to their chin. They did not have lips so their razor sharp, dagger like teeth were exposed in a permanent macabre grin.

They started wearing masks when they began interacting more often with live family members of the dead they'd come to collect, after literally frightening enough people to death you would too. Teagan had seen Siobhan often enough that the novelty of what her mask covered had worn off and The Banshee was comfortable au naturel. All Banshees, at least the ones Teagan had encountered, had waist length purple hair, grey eyes, flawless ivory skin and a bone thin build. They were immensely strong despite their slightness and their purpose in the world usually kept them from harm; they were women who had kept their virtue in life and passed away before losing the purity of their souls. The goddess Morrigan commissioned them to guide the souls of the dead to wherever they were destined afterward; they kept track of their charges in a ledger that was rumored to be bound with Mermaid skin and taxied them to the hereafter in what is known as Coiste Bodhar or, Death Coach. Their Death Coaches are driven by members of the UnSeelie Court known as The Dullahan or, Headless Horseman; malevolent Folk not to be trifled with who lacked The Banshees dark humor or, any humor for that matter. Teagan was glad they stayed atop the coaches they drove and kept their heads under their arms where they could not speak.

"Let me see your ledger," Teagan asked without preamble, clicking the print button on her computer so she could turn in her report of the evening's events before she left.

"Skip right over the small talk why don't you," Siobhan folded her hands on her lap.

"I need to know who you just collected," Teagan pressed.

"No," Siobhan chuckled.

"Let me see your ledger, please," Teagan smiled.

"No," Siobhan responded, the mirth gone from her voice.

"Siobhan, you know I wouldn't ask if I didn't really need it," Teagan plead.

"You know the only Folk who see the ledger aside from The Banshee are The Laoch at the Gates of Tearmanhalla and Tearmancnoc," Siobhan was referring to the Warriors who stood guard at Haven Hall and Haven Hill; they were essentially bouncers of the afterlife. The Laoch were male Folk who had served honorably as soldiers during their lifetime and were willing to keep the souls of the departed safe for the rest of eternity; they didn't need to be pure, just valiant. Haven Hall was merely a VIP room, for those Folk who so chose, to commiserate before they moved on to Feanlaurel. Feanlaurel or, Faerie Haven, was where they all existed weather coming or going. It was where they began and where Bel and Danu, the Father and Mother of them all respectively, lived and kept watch over all their children.

Haven Hill was somewhat of a purgatory for those wayward souls who had chosen to feed the darkness in themselves instead of the light; every now and then they had a mutiny and a few would sneak back into the world to exact revenge or, cause mayhem purely out of spite. They usually ended up as Brownies, Kelpies or, Succubi and were welcomed with open wings into The Winter Court; many of them took over bodies of human politicians and relished changing political party affiliation for their own amusement.

"Maybe if you just happened to drop it on my desk and it fell open to the page I need," Teagan suggested.

"Still no but, that was a good try," Siobhan chuckled softly at Teagan's weak attempt.

"If I guess correctly, could you tell me?"

"There's no harm in guessing I suppose," Siobhan looked down slyly, brushing a non-existent piece of dust off her coat.

"First, I need to know a few things."

"Very well, if I can answer I will," The Banshee nodded.

"Does a soul need to be complete for you to collect it?"

"No."

"When a Reaver dies, what happens to the souls they've consumed?"

"They have a choice."

"To stay or, go?"

"Yes."

"Does a soul have to be complete to stay?"

"You really don't deal with humans very often do you," Siobhan's eyebrows raised in amusement.

"I'll take that for a no, then."

"Correct."

"What if their body is gone?"

"Then they have no choice but, to go."

"Can Reaver's take an incomplete soul?"

"Were you not listening about humans?"

"That'll be a yes, then?"

"Yes," Siobhan nodded.

"Does it matter how long the soul has been parted from the body?"

"No."

"Did Blair Phillips stay or, go?"

"Yes," The Banshee's eyes twinkled.

"Is he still known by that name?"

"We are all known by many names."

Teagan let the information sink in a bit and thought about what she would ask next; how far she could push Siobhan before putting her off. Siobhan stared at her from across the desk; waiting for the next question patiently as if she were being interviewed for a job.

"What will happen to Velika," Teagan inquired.

"She will go where she is meant to," The Banshee responded flatly, Teagan knew she was cutting close to her boundary.

"Orion Red Birch is safe?"

"Orion Red Birch is not your concern."

"Are your ledgers really made with Mermaid skin," Teagan gave in to her curiosity.

"Anything else," Siobhan asked, chuckling as she reached to put her gloves on.

"How long has Tylane Dekawley been dead?"

"Anything else," Siobhan repeated humorlessly.

"No and thank you for indulging me," Teagan rose from her chair to open the door; Siobhan followed her lead.

"You're welcome princess," she nodded and stood at the threshold, "until next time; may the Death Coach circle thrice before taking you home."

"And may the souls you gather bring naught but, honor."

Siobhan secured her mask and left swiftly and silently down the hall, leaving Teagan to digest the revelation that an enemy long presumed dead was likely very much alive and if that were true, she needed to plan her next move accordingly.

Strike

The smell of wet oak trees permeated his senses as he trudged through the wash behind their home. Reaching out a hand to brush the leaves as he passed them, he took a deep breath to steady his heart that threatened to burst through his chest with each pulse. He stopped at the bottom of the hill, in his mind's eye he continued on up toward the house; whitewashed walls greeting him when he approached, stairs creaking under his weight.

He could nearly feel the weight of the heavy handle in his grip when he opened the front door. She was standing in the kitchen at the counter singing "Green sleeves" and kneading dough; almond flour streaked across her porcelain skin and in her long black hair. He breathes her in; Cinnamon, Caraway and Orange peel fills his lungs, she is making Soda bread for supper that night. The house is comfortably quiet; this memory is before children. When it was just the two of them and not the family of seven they would later become; this was a time he most loved. He did not have to share his wife's affections or, play the bad guy; a time when he was not so self-conscious about his grey hair or, the scars on his chest. She had saved him though she did not know it and he would never tell her; he could never tell her or, she might be taken from him and that was not something he would allow. She was everything that mattered and made him human; everything that was good and pure.

She was everything he was not and he loved her as much as what little soul he had left was capable of; she turns toward him, her bright smile lighting up the already well lit house. Then it's gone; the dough, her smile, the angelic voice. He feels the door handle again as the door slams shut on him, opens his eyes and he is still standing at the bottom of the hill; presently knee deep in muddy water. A single tear darkens his pale lashes and falls into the murky wash below him; steeling his resolve, he makes his way to the home his wife had been running by herself for the past four months. Dreading the conversation he is about to have, he clings to the joy that leaves him with each passing moment.

Blair Nathaniel Davies had only been called that for the past hundred years of his life. He was not born Faerie and still was not sure exactly what he was aside from content on any other day but, this one. Hawthorne, one of his most beloved authors once wrote, "No man, for any considerable period, can wear one face to himself and another to the multitude, without finally getting bewildered as to which one is true." That comment could well have been written about himself; to his family he was loving husband, stern father and exemplary salesman. To his Queen he was loyal servant, occasional lover and sadistic errand boy. He felt no qualms about either mask he bore; he quite liked each of his roles in equal measure. He enjoyed his family life and relished his secret life in The Queens employ, though The Queen would say his secret life was that of family man and that his true place was as her subject.

One hundred years of this dual life had found him bewildered finally but, only because the remaining piece of his soul had found its way back to him. He had died in a pub in 1912 or, at least the first version of himself had; he had been Blair Nathaniel Phillips then and his greatest desire was to end his life. He had invested poorly and amassed enormous debt during his tenure as a Conductor with The Southern Pacific Railroad. The west was still very wild back then and it was just as easy to lose one's wages at a saloon as it was to burn the skin off your hand in a smelter. It was in one of these saloons he had overheard some of his coworkers gossiping over a card game about strange happenings in a brothel they all frequented. According to the inebriated degenerates, the Madame of the brothel was some sort of Vampire, whatever that was, and for the right price a man could live forever; though in those days that seemed more a curse than a blessing; days on end of dirty work in hot sweaty weather for little pay was not appealing to Blair at all and he couldn't imagine why it would appeal to anyone else either. He wouldn't mind a night with the Madame though. She was unlike anything Blair had seen in all his twenty four years; nearly white blonde hair, big dark eyes, tall and slender. Yes, Blair could definitely go for at least one night with the Madame of The Black Canary and three nights after he overheard that conversation he would get just that.

He had finally reached his former residence. He could smell fresh chocolate chip cookies through the open kitchen window and realized it was Thursday, his wife would be baking treats for their youngest son's post football practice snack.

She always made enough for the entire team and the lot of them usually stayed for dinner. It had been four months since he had been home for dinner or, seen his family for that matter. He knew this would be the last time he would look upon his wife's face and was grateful for the adjusted perspective his missing piece had given him; grateful and resentful because he knew it would not last. The copper gate winked at him in the afternoon sun and the heat it had absorbed nearly burnt his hand when he pushed his way through it; the hinges grated against themselves and he was reminded of yet another task he had failed to complete before leaving his family. It was the first time in a long time he had felt failure, the first time in a century that he had felt ambivalence; he remembered now why he had craved suicide so long ago. Raising his hand to knock on the front door Teagan and Rylan had gifted them, he hesitated momentarily; the red hi gloss like a warning for what was to come. The onslaught of questions and insufficient answers he would respond to them with. The partially healed wounds he would rip open and pour salt into just by being present. He thought of turning back but, only shook the idea from his mind after much deliberation; the desire of seeing his wife once more outweighed his cowardice. He knocked three times and waited for her to answer; when she did his stomach dropped through the concrete they stood on as she dried her hands on an apron their eldest daughter had made her for mother's day a decade ago. She turned on her heel and walked back down the hall to the kitchen, leaving him standing in the wake of his favorite of her sundresses.

"Are you going to invite me in," he asked after her.

"So, its vampire you've turned the last four months and cannot enter unless bidden," she called back.

"No, I didn't think I should just waltz in," he responded stepping across the threshold tentatively.

"It is still *your* house Blair, if that is your real name," she responded flatly.

"Not anymore it isn't."

"The name or, the house?"

"Both."

"Why is that exactly," she hissed through gritted teeth as he rounded the corner.

"I will explain but, we do not have much time and I do wish you'd put down the knife," he requested as she finished an expert julienne of tomatoes for individual pizzas the kids would make later.

"Right, sorry."

"May I have a whiskey while I explain," he requested as he sat heavily on a stool at their breakfast bar.

"Neat?"

"Of course."

"It's good to know some things never change," she took his favorite bottle from the freezer; already half empty from her putting it to good use in his absence.

"Tyffani, you know I love you right?"

"I use to think that was unambiguous but, some things *do* change."

"That never has," he whispered taking his glass as she slid it across the counter to him; she had been a bar tender while she completed University and had never lost her touch.

"Please get to the explaining. I have heard awful things these last few months and I would love to hear your side; understand that whatever your reasoning may be, we are through. You are gone and as far as the children know you were killed in the explosion at the hospital."

"My children think I am dead," he swallowed his liquor hard; bitterer now than it ever had been.

"Why shouldn't they? The father they knew and loved does not sit before me, you are not the man I married and they do not need to know that evil may run through their veins."

"They are half you, they could never be evil, you are pure enough to counter even a Winter poison," he smiled sadly into his whiskey tumbler.

"I think I'll join you in the drink," she said, repeating her motions from seconds before but, filling her glass twice as full.

His somber yellow eyes looked up at her through light grey lashes, searching for any trace of what she might be thinking. When her poker face stayed true, he took another sip before setting into his insufficient explanation.

"I was not always as you have known me, this is not my first life and I'm certainly not deserving of any. You know me as Blair Nathaniel Davies, others call me Kaius; my true name is Blair Nathaniel Phillips and I was born on the floor of a train car in the California desert to poor immigrant English parents during the spring of 1888. My father was a rail worker and my mother washed sheets at a factory. They both died when I was 8 and I took up the work my mother did so I could live on my own and not end up in an orphanage or, worse. I wanted a better life than the one I was born into but, sixteen years after his death I was no better off than my father; a railway man just as he had been though, I had advanced to conductor. It wasn't enough for my greedy young self so I started placing bets on anything that could be bet upon. I won often, I lost more often and soon I started owing a lot of people a lot of money. When I couldn't settle up, they took remuneration wherever and whenever they could. I ended up being an enforcer for the Maudlin gang at night and worked my days away on the rail; eventually it all became too much and I decided to end my sorry existence."

"You were human then," she had made her way to the stool next to his and sipped slowly on her beverage, drinking in his words behind her still expressionless face.

"I was human. I still might be. I am not entirely sure on that one and neither of us will ever get an answer to that I'm afraid," he shrugged and sipped before beginning again.

"You were still in California?"

"No, no I had made my way to Bisbee when I was about twenty and traveled across Southwest Arizona for work; by my twenty fourth year I had made Sahuarita my home base. It's not what it once was but, back in 1912 it was still fairly new and very beautiful. I ended up at The Ornery Rattle-snake, a saloon near Tombstone, one night after a long day of work and overheard some of my coworkers speaking about a strange woman who managed the brothel down the street; the rumors were that she was some sort of demon who could make a man immortal and all powerful, provided he paid the proper price.

Of course I wanted to see this demon woman for myself and as luck would have it, she saw fit to grace us with her presence that night; she had come in to drum up some business for her girls."

"My husband, the bustle hunter," Tyffani rolled her eyes.

"I was not your husband then and that version of me would never get to be your husband darling," he reached for her hand.

"Go on," she recoiled at his gesture and sat stick straight on her stool.

"She was the loveliest thing I had ever seen, she called herself Katia and looked every inch the Russian Princess that name would suggest. The first night she told me that what I wanted could be done and quoted me what I'm sure she deemed a fair amount; my soul was all she asked for. I assumed she was just being cryptic of course and agreed to it without hesitation, all the misdeeds I'd partaken in I assumed I hadn't a soul left anyways.

We set a meeting for three nights from then, I was to go alone to a pub in Tucson called The Red Lantern; your friends own that property and the pub is now known as Collin's Brewery," he paused for a sip of whiskey, there were only a few gulps left of it now and his wife did not move to refresh his beverage as she usually would.

The reality of his situation was becoming clearer with each piece of his story, this next part was not one he relished telling.

"I did as she asked, arrived early even and ordered us drinks. She had barely removed her gloves when a large man burst through the door like a crack of lightning, his steel grey eyes set on me immediately and before I could push her out of the way she was gone. I remember a sharp pain at the back of my head and then everything went black. The next thing I knew everything was illuminated, blinding white light forced my eyes shut and my nose was burned by a fierce sulfur stench. I couldn't breathe, couldn't see and my limbs felt like they were made of lead; I felt like I was drowning and burning all at once. Then I heard the sweetest voice speaking the strangest language, I felt excruciating pain in my chest for what seemed like ages and then it stopped suddenly, after a while I heard Katia's voice speaking the same language as the first voice but, more fervently and different somehow. I'm not sure how long I was lying there but, when I eventually woke up I felt like a dog who'd been wrung through a washer; everywhere ached, I still couldn't breathe properly and I was blind in one eye. I was on a gurney in the morgue of Bansail Hospital."

"God, oh god it was me. I was the first voice you heard," realization ripped across Tyffani's face; she leaned forward, elbows on the counter, head in her hands and began to shake. Hot tears rolled down her flushed cheeks and pooled on the cold black granite in front of her.

"Katia was the second. I know now that was not her real name, she was the Soul Reaver Augustana Von Dotch and Madame Katia was merely a hobby of sorts. Even Reaver's need to make money I suppose or, maybe she was just bored, either way, the magic you attempted ruined the magic she attempted and I was driven insane. The only reason I am privy to these memories now is because she died today and the piece of my soul she managed to obtain was released back to me, I wish she had taken it all or, that I had died during either attempt to garner it."

"Either attempt? I only tried to save you, not steal your soul," Tyffani hiccupped through her tears.

"Right," Blair nodded agreement, "the second attempt was made by The Winter Queen. After I snuck out of the hospital she found me wandering half blind and equally naked through the woods, she offered to finish what Augustana had started and I foolishly begged her to do so. She took what was left of me, named me Kaius and when she was done I had changed physically as well; my black hair turned grey, my dark eyes now a mustard yellow and I had gained a bit of height and weight as well. The last bit I wasn't so upset about," he chuckled quietly.

"That's why I didn't recognize you," Tyffani sniffled into the corner of her apron.

"Yes but, I was drawn to you. Without realizing it, you left your mark on me and a bit of my old self was left with you as well. The Queen wanted me to spy on your family and I did that. She wanted me to get you to fall in love with me, to marry me; I did that as well. What I did not anticipate was falling in love with you," he smiled at her as he wiped tears from her puffy eyes.

"You're just saying that," she scoffed.

"No. You are easy to love my Tyffani Ann. You are the best woman I know. Any part of me that is or, ever was any good at all is because of you. Any positive thing I have ever felt in any of my wretched lives is because of you. You are the strongest woman I know and I want you never to forget that. Promise me you will never forget that," he insisted, holding her hands in his and kissing the back of each in turn.

"Promise," she whispered.

"Please also understand that the next time you see me, if there is a next time, I will not be Blair. I will be Kaius and only Kaius, The Queen will steal the rest of my soul when I return to her and I *must* return to her or, she will come for you and I cannot have that. She is hungry in all manner of that word, she will take your soul, the souls of our children and the soul of anyone who finds themselves in her megalomaniacal path. There is no good in her and I don't think there ever was," he finished eyes closed and brow furrowed.

"This is it then?"

"Yes, this is it."

"What will I tell the children then?"

"They already think I am dead?"

"Yes."

"Ah Fiona's Wings, six broken hearts you have to mend. I am so sorry my love," he wiped a tear from her cheeks with his thumb.

"Why did we have five children," she jested.

"Sounded like a good idea at the time? Besides, they hadn't invented cable yet."

"True," she sighed heavily, "they are devastated but, young hearts heal quickly and they are a perseverant lot."

"They are crazy," he chuckled, "that little one? I am pretty sure he's all me, sorry about that."

"That he is and I am glad to have him, even with his inherited eccentricities."

"Tell them to treat others as they would like to be treated and to brush their teeth twice a day. Tell Sydni and Savannah to respect themselves always, to allow themselves to be taken care of by a good man and to smile every day; our daughters have the loveliest smiles. Tell Bryce to use his head more often and not follow others so much, remind LT there's more to life than the party and tell Gaige that his best is always enough and that there is a bigger picture than even the adults in his life may know. Tell them I loved them every day that I was privileged enough to be called their father, tell them they are good because of their mother and that I will be proud of them no matter what they choose to be as long as it is true to who they are."

"I will tell them that."

"Thank you. I must go now. Be strong," he took her hand and kissed it before exiting the back of the house, leaving her to finish preparing dinner and to steel herself against what was coming next.

Posture

There are four possible responses in the brain when confronted with attack; Flight, fight, posture and submit. When he and Teagan were attacked while leaving the hospital, he had chosen to fight, now it was time for posturing.

If it was Rylan they were after, they would have to chase after him. He had learned more than a few tricks about meditation metaphysics and how the mind works from his wife, and the research he had done for his own pleasure during his twelve decades on the planet. He intended to use every bit he could recall, to antagonize whatever monster had come for his family. Hide and seek. He would be the bait, lead this hungry bloodhound as far away and be as distracting as possible to whoever it was. Lion's Breath. Stasis. Teagan always moved a mile a minute, her brain was always so busy that she needed to move her body equally as busily and he reminded her often to take a deep breath. Exhale and inhale in equal measure. In through the nose, release your tongue from the room of your mouth. Unclench your jaw. Breathe.

Teagan had taught him how to manage their connection after he had come home from war. She had to work to get into his head, she didn't with others, he had always been very pleased about this; it annoyed Teagan endlessly. Once they had practiced enough it was like a switch, terribly convenient at parties when they wanted to leave and needed to synchronize their goodbyes.

The person chasing him around his own head was not the person who had attacked them. It didn't really matter; Teagan would kill them both. He wanted so badly to let her know it was Tylane. Everyone thought she was dead, here she was introducing herself and trying to seduce him. He had never been inclined toward weak women and was not about to start now. Besides, Tegan would have his guts for garters if he had even a metaphysical affair. Sharing had never been her strong suit. Giving, sure. Sharing? Not a chance. Her sisters had ruined that for her.

Tylane was unhinged, "cheese has slid all the way off her cracker," as his father liked to say. She reeked of desperation and like any hungry animal was becoming increasingly careless. She did not have Teagan's gift. If you knew Teagan Inez Patrick McCarthy was in your head, it was because she wanted you to know. The finesse and grace with which she moved was unmatched by any creature, on any plane. Certainly, the butcher currently trying to get him to unlock the door his wife was on the other side of lacked finesse or grace and seemed to simmer in frustration, a bitter steep for all involved. Let's go on a ride along then, shall we? Lovely.

"Ugh gods I will be so glad to be done with my first year solo so I can stop chasing my own ass around the desert," Teagan grumbled at him.

"Testing the newbie is a time-honored tradition, be grateful they respect you enough to put you to task and not give you an easy out just because of who you are," Rylan chuckled at her exasperation.

He could feel her rolling her eyes at him. Some days he lived to annoy her, it was so easy to do and some of the most fun they could have with their clothes on. She appreciated him annoying her, even if she never said it out loud, it was a mark of them being equals that had the ability to annoy her.

"I think they're all too scared to treat me differently," she was walking them through an area typically used for hunting, there had been reports of beasts being eaten by a mountain lion. Well, the public had been assured it was a mountain lion and that said mountain lion would be dispatched humanely. Game and Fish had contacted FLEC to investigate after a hunter scouting the area interrupted a creature feasting on one of their agents. Poor woman had to have her memory erased by the flame haired fae currently leading Rylan toward the scene of the crime.

They would fast track her, which she appreciated and resented equally. She knew her ability was unique and useful, and she didn't want to be stuck trudging through the desert in the middle of the night forever, but she still believed she needed to earn good things, and this was how she'd earn being a detective.

"I kind of like midnight shift," she whispered aloud, "I sleep while you are at work, we get to have dinner together and I can do my own thing midweek during days off. It's not so bad, you know?"

"I knew you'd tire of sleeping next to me at some point, I just didn't realize it would be so soon," he teased.

"Oh, I do love having the bed all to myself four sleeps a

week," she teased back, "it's almost as a good as the cramped dorm room I had to share during the academy."

Her poor classmates at the academy were no match for Teagan, she basically used them to perfect what she had been doing her whole life; being in other minds and influencing their thoughts to varying degrees of detriment. It was mostly innocent of course, she was a being of integrity, she did not hesitate however, to encourage those who wanted authority for their own gain to decide magical law enforcement just wasn't the right fit for them after all.

Having come from a big family sharing space was not necessarily an issue, though having had her own home for the decade prior to her foray into a life of service set her expectation of cleanliness much higher than was reasonable for most. The issue was being immersed with so many others en masse without much of a break. So many different energies at play presented a challenge she had not yet been met with, she had to learn how to regulate her emotions and communicate in a way she had never been forced to before and the first few months of weekends at home were spent on opposite ends of the house. He had never held it against her, wasn't smug or condescending, Rylan cooked for them, made tea and spent time in his shop, hammering away his own anxieties. He could feel her frustration at being overstimulated without joining her in her head, a bitter steep for them both. He remembered what that felt like, he did not deal with it as well as she had and told her as much.

He spent many a night holding her while she cried, hot, angry tears that left her pale skin swollen and red, brine crusted when she awoke each Sunday. Her fathers French

Toast recipe wasn't a prescription but, it was somewhat of a cure-all for Teagan, it always had been. Rylan prepared it for her breakfast enthusiastically and as often as she'd allow. He washed her hair for her, brushed and braided it. She swore he was better at braiding than she was but, he knew she found it comforting and that she appreciated him taking care of her. He was one of the only people she allowed to take care of her, he'd worked damn hard to earn that privilege.

Now they found themselves mid-winter in the Arizona desert, just before witching hour, tracking an exiled Wendigo who had inspired deer to eat each other, when the creature itself was not feasting on them. The stench wafting toward them on the chill whisper of wind announced the Wendigo's presence before they were near. Rylan was glad they were down wind, so the announcement was not the other way around. Wendigos are nasty and Teagan would have to be quick to trick it before it tried to do the same. She started the moment the hot garbage smell smacked her in the face, Rylan could see the faint shimmer ahead indicating she had set up a glamour. They continued on in silence, it took every ounce of will to keep from gagging at the rottenness issuing from the tree line ahead. He had only smelled it's like one other time and there were trenches involved in that instance. He pulled away from his own memory of rotting death just in time to catch Teagan's signal to stop. What appeared to be a bipedal deer was kneeling over a lump of what Rylan could only assume was its most recent kill. There was blood beginning to congeal on paddles of cactus nearby, and the creature was squealing and moaning alternately around mouthfuls of gore.

Teagan had consulted a friend in the north who was

familiar with Wendigos, how to approach and dispatch them. There could be no negotiating, Wendigos only knew malice and hunger and it was satiating one of those needs presently. Their hearts were ice, literally, so to rid the world of a Wendigo you need only break their heart, how poetic. The Bard would be proud.

She was quick indeed. Macabre as it was Rylan enjoyed watching Teagan work. Silent as she approached from above on her wings, oh how he loved her wings, iridescent and soft, like gossamer spun feathers, she dropped with equal silence, her sai stabbing right through the Wendigos back, just under the left shoulder blade. It froze, almost comically, and tried to twist around to see who its assassin was. Human facial features fixed into a would be scream, neon blue shards of ice and purple blood sprayed from its breast as Teagan's weapon shoved through, crunching through bones, lungs squelching out their last bits of oxygen.

Teagan landed gracefully, immediately setting about burning the corpse now leaking blood and ice where it was felled. Rylan moved to assist, he gathered whatever detritus he could find in the nearby desert, not a difficult task this far into winter, and brought it back to Teagan who had just finished removing the rack of antlers from its head. They piled all of it, actual deer, Wendigo and the antlers that had recently been parted from it, atop what Rylan had gathered, and set it all ablaze. The fire flashed blue-white momentarily before catching in earnest and they stayed until it burned itself out. Burning body stench is preferable to hot garbage, trench death stench.

Flight, fight, posture, submit.

Time Bender

When she arrived back at the station at the end of her day, she was so immersed in thoughts about what she might have for dinner she nearly blew right past her office. She paused just near the threshold, realizing the door was open already, when she was sure she had left it closed and locked.

The light was on, someone else had figured out the dimmer switch, sitting on her couch, one long leg crossed over the other, was a dark-haired man she had only ever heard stories about.

"Andreaus," she hesitated, "did you let yourself in?"
"No," he stood to greet her as she entered, "a gaggle of your fellow officers made sure I found my way."

His hand was warm when he took hers, nodding as he did. The frequency of his very being hummed with adventure. He truly was everywhere and nowhere, even as he stood before her.

"Of course they did," she rolled her eyes as she turned to close the door, "they all have crushes on you."

"Do they really," his dark eyebrows shot upward, "well I am off romance at the moment, but I will certainly keep that in mind."

"Please don't, cops are a nightmare to date."

"Who said anything about dating," he winked.

"Fair enough," Teagan pulled a notebook from her top drawer, "while I am surprised to see you, your being here is rather convenient."

"Ah, about that," he shifted on the couch, "rumors of my body count have been greatly exaggerated."

"I can check, you know," she leveled a withering look at his too handsome face.

"No, I don't believe you can," no jest in his grey eyes.

She grinned so wide nearly all her teeth showed, then immediately frowned. She tried to tip toe through his mind and found herself rebuffed instantly. Gratefully, it was not painful, just surprising. She tried again, only to be met with the same result. Andreaus sat before her, grinning just as she had been only moments before.

"How?"

"I honestly do not know," he exhaled forcefully, "it is just a perk of being me, I suppose. The gods knew it would be too dangerous for anyone else to be traipsing around in there."

"Old fashioned way it is then," Teagan took a steeling breath and took the cap off her pen.

"Teagan," Andreaus said gently, "I am very sorry for what happened to your family."

"Thank you," it was a near robotic response anymore, "we'll get through it. What do you know about the murder of Orion Redbirch?"

"Not where I thought we'd begin," Andreaus frowned, "I know nothing of that murder."

"You took no part in it whatsoever?"

"No, I am not in the business of murdering elves."

"Who are you in the business of murdering, then?"

"No one," he looked at the floor, "not for many years."

"Who was the last person you murdered?"

"What day is it," he asked seriously.

She looked at her calendar and realized that it had been so long since she had properly questioned someone, she had left out all the preamble.

"It is Monday August 7th, 2006 at," she checked her phone, "1622, Arizona time."

"Given that time is a construct, the last person I murdered has not technically been born yet."

"Why did you come in today?"

"To let you know I had no part in what happened to your family," his face sorrowful.

"I did not think you had," she eyed him cautiously.

"An old friend got word to me that my name had been mixed in with the current goings on," he chose his words carefully.

"Which friend?"

Andreaus only shook his head no, in response.

"You keep saying family and not husband, why?"

"Because you all were attacked," he glanced at her swollen midsection.

"What do you know about Tylane DeKawley?"

Andreaus shifted in his seat again, uncrossing his legs, folding his hands together in his lap.

"I know that right now, today, she is not as dead as she's successfully lead everyone to believe."

"We are what we are," she looked him directly in the eye, "enough faerie quadrille around the truth."

He held her gaze, thought for a full thrum of heartbeats and said, "she is not dead."

Click

After dropping off her paperwork, Teagan waited impatiently outside her Sergeants office for someone to escort her home, this was the most inconvenient thing about being back to work post assault. Depending on the day and time she was coming or going, a different TAC Squad officer was available for escort; 1630 hours on a Thursday it would probably be Galen or West. West Henley was a mild mannered, simply humored young officer. He was the only Sylph Teagan had ever met. His mother was a Knowme, his father a Kelpie and both were dead. The only Kelpie she had encountered was a nasty piece of work and she had heard terrible stories about them dragging children to their deaths, she wondered if West's gentle nature hid some dark compulsion he had inherited. He was a full head taller than Teagan, had closely cropped black hair and bright green eyes; just like the other men in his unit, he was a former soldier and had kept up with the rigorous physical regimen learned of that profession. The handsome Sylph himself had just rounded the corner and smiled broadly at her, Teagan was relieved he had forgiven her scarring the right cheek of his otherwise perfect visage not long ago.

"Afternoon Detective McCarthy," he greeted her brightly.

"Good afternoon, West," she shook his hand firmly.

"I see your six pack just keeps growing," he gingerly touched her belly.

"I doubt I'll ever have one of those again," she smiled sadly.

"Maybe not but, you'll have a healthy sprite instead and that's more important," he reassured her, smiling kindly.

"Thank you, I'm sure that's true," she nodded agreement.

"Alright then Teagan, ready to go?"

"Yes sir," she responded, following his lead toward the employee entrance at the back of the FLEC building.

"Correct me if I'm wrong but, this is the first time I've taken you home yes," he asked her once they had reached the exit door.

"Yes, I believe it is," she responded after thinking a moment.

"Good to know my memory is as sharp as ever," he chuckled and then looked at her very seriously.

"West is everything alright," the concern in her voice further straining the look on his face.

"You know what I am?"

"I know you are Sylph," she nodded; confusion furrowing her brow.

"Do you know what that means?"

"You are the only one I've met so, probably not explain, please? You are worrying me."

"No need to worry detective, it just means that I am an air elemental and when I fly all you will see is a wisp of cloud where my body should be," he tried mustering a hearty smile to cover his self-consciousness.

"Seriously?"

"Yeah," he nodded.

"Do not be embarrassed about that, that's one of the cleverest things I've ever heard. I'm kind of jealous actually."

"Really," he brightened.

"Yes. I mean I could do it but, it would take a lot of energy to project that kind of thing."

"Well, thank you," he smiled broadly, putting his flying goggles on.

"Time to fly," she said, putting her sunglasses on and mentally preparing herself for the journey home, "see you when we land."

Pixie and Sylph landed safely at the back of the McCarthy property after a brief, uneventful flight, there weren't even any planes in the air for them to toy with.

"Thank you for the escort home, West. Will you be going back to work now?"

"In a manner of speaking, I am to relieve Sergeant Murphy," he informed her.

"I see. Well, if you late shift guys need anything just give us a holler at the house and be safe, please."

"Yes ma'am," he nodded acknowledgement and left to find Galen, wherever his post was that day.

They had a system in place Teagan was sure but, it was given out strictly on a need-to-know basis, all Teagan needed to know was that she was protected round the clock by some of the most elite soldiers she had the privilege of calling friends.

Teagan heard her father's guitar before she entered through the back door of her home and shook her head at once again being robbed of a moment alone. She was grateful and knew it was necessary but, she could hardly shower in peace these days. She would be glad when Rylan woke up and everyone could resume their normal routines. She loved her family immensely but, missed the quiet time she reveled in after a long day of work, the large cup of hot tea she could tuck into while Rylan cooked dinner and sang to her from the kitchen, the cool shower she would relish after such a long sweaty August day, the dreamless sleep on their unfairly comfortable bed, in their never cool enough these days bedroom. No, Rylan could not wake up soon enough and she hoped she had finally puzzled together the pieces that would lead her to helping him do just that.

"Father! Airioch! I'm home," she called from the kitchen.

'Teagan! How was work?'

'Hello Airioch. Work was educational.'

'Oh? How so?'

'Could you see something that I am remembering?'

'Perhaps...let's try it.'

Teagan thought of the last time her family had gotten together at their parent's house for dinner, specifically when her sister's husband Blair chuffed at her being unable to play Schwoozle.

'That man, he works for The Queen. Why do you know him Teagan,' Airioch inquired suspiciously, backing away from her where she stood on the kitchen table.

'It's alright. Well, it's not really, that's my brother-in-law.'

'Kaius is your brother-in-law?! I thought I could trust you!'

'You can, Airioch! You can. Please, sit, let me explain.'

'Please do so quickly,' she snorted a puff of smoke menacingly.

"Teagan? You alright out there," her father called from her bedroom.

"*Yes sir, I'll be there in just a moment,*' she responded, realizing after the fact that she had forgotten to do so out loud.

'*He attacked Rylan and me at the hospital, he's been missing ever since.*'

'*You think he murdered Orion,*' she asked after taking a moment to decide that Teagan was telling the truth.

'*Yes, I think he may have been instructed to.*'

'*Instructed?*'

'*He wouldn't have done so of his own accord, he is the Queens puppet.*'

'*She has many.*'

'*Did Orion ever mention anywhere Kaius may have stayed when he wasn't with the Queen?*'

'*No,*' she answered after thinking it over.

'*Would you remember how to get to the Queen's hill?*'

'*I do remember but, you have to have been in to get in.*'

'*How do you mean?*'

'*You must give blood to enter her mound.*'

'*And your blood must be recognized to do so.*'

'*Yes.*'

'*Well, that is an old Faerie trick. She is more sadistic than I gave her credit for,*' Teagan sighed disappointment.

'*I'm sorry,*' Airioch's little head hung low.

'*Do not apologize, you have been more of a help than I could ever repay.*'

'*Really?*'

'*Really,*' Teagan smiled at her and stroked the soft scales on her horned nose.

'You are too kind Princess McCarthy.'
'We'll see about that, follow me would you? I have a favor to ask.'
'Of course, anything!'

Airioch crawled up Teagan's arm to sit atop her left shoulder, her preferred perch, and they made their way back to the bedroom where her father sat playing a Spanish melody on his guitar.

"Hello my father," Teagan greeted him enthusiastically, taking a seat on the edge of her bed near Rylan's feet, "how is our patient doing today?"

"Hello my Teagan, our patient remains unchanged," he said as brightly as his grey mood allowed, studying her face from his position on Rylan's chair.

"I figured as much," she sighed and looked over at her sleeping beauty, "I have a favor to ask."

"Certainly, anything," the King responded without missing a chord.

"I need you to memory share with Airioch."

"That's easy enough."

"I need you to remember Tylane."

His longer than the rest of his digits thumb nail clipped the nylon string he was strumming a bit too sharply and it snapped, he moved his head back just in time to avoid getting popped in the eye.

"You need me to what," the joy in his voice evaporated.

"I need you to remember Tylane."

"I've no pleasant memories with her my daughter," he said flatly.

"That seems to be a common theme," Teagan took a deep

breath and took her father's right hand in both of hers, "Please da."

"You will explain later," he instructed as he put down his guitar.

"Yes," she nodded agreement without hesitation.

Airioch go to the King, read his thoughts if you can but, try to focus on the voices he is projecting.

'I will try.'

'He is an excellent projector,' Teagan assured the anxious Feandragoon.

"She is ready Father," Teagan told him as soon as Airioch was settled in his hand and had given her a nod of approval, "try to remember something with her speaking, I will not be part of this if I don't need to be so share away and be patient with each other."

Teagan left the two to their work and crawled up to snuggle with her husband. She closed her eyes and drank in his smell, he still smelled like Rylan. She placed her hand on his chest, his heart was still beating its normal rhythm. She pushed into his mind like she had at least thrice a day since the accident, he was still paused on his last thought of 'family.' She sighed heavily and tried to relax her body, 'start with your toes' her father had taught each of his children when they were young. She wiggled the swollen toes of her swollen feet and had only just begun lamenting their size when she was ripped from her reverie by two shouts; Airioch's shot across her mind, her father's cracked the silence of the room like cannon fire. Airioch leaped from The King's palm and landed roughly on Teagan's belly.

'That's her,' Airioch thought so forcefully Teagan's head began to throb.

"Well father," she sat up slowly, gently stroking the visibly frightened Feandragoon, "it would seem Tylane is not as dead as we thought."

"Yes dear about that," he started as Teagan scooted off of the bed and over to her wardrobe.

"What about it father," she sighed from the effort of moving her pregnant body from its previously comfortable position, "is this like your sending Orion in as a spy and not telling me about it?"

"That's not, that wasn't," a gob smacked Timothy Patrick tripped over his weak excuse.

"No it wasn't and now he isn't so if you don't mind I've got to change," she said over her shoulder after shutting the wardrobe door harder than was necessary, "work attire isn't acceptable for ripping your eldest sibling a new asshole."

"Teagan please let me explain," he said softly from the other side of the bathroom door that had just been closed in his face.

"I don't have time," she called through the t-shirt she was struggling to pull over her head.

"You must make time Rua, please."

"No," she huffed as she opened the door, "stay here, I'll be home soon and you can explain then."

"Teagan please?!"

"No," she turned in her tracks to glare directly at him, "I need to point my anger in the right direction. You can explain later."

"It may be too late then," he said quietly, slumping back

into the chair he had claimed as his own since Rylan wasn't available to argue 'seat backs.'

"Then it is too late! Everything these days is *too late* father. I must go take care of some business but, I will be home shortly, stop acting like a petulant child, my stars!"

'Airioch stay here with my gentlemen please.'

'Must I? I don't like you going out alone and besides The King is here.'

'Yes, you must. I need you to protect Rylan and The King should it come to it.'

'I don't like it.'

'I know but, I need to know they are safe and you're the best way of that.'

'You be safe. You and that little one are the only reason I am still here.'

'I know,' she ran a finger softly down Airioch's soft belly a few times to help soothe her.

'That's not fair,' the Feandragoon hummed delight.

'I know. Call me if anything happens, I'll see you soon.'

Fire

Teagan's temper matched that of an Aos Si denied an offering; had her sister owed her for a Faerie mound she'd have set it afire from the safety of her office and sat back with a pack of marshmallows to roast on the flames. She hoped for her sister's sake that Danu looked well upon her today, for she was tempted to bring Siobhan with her and cut out the middle Fae. It took no time to reach the Davies house from her own with the Princess McCarthy in such a rage and she found herself banging on the red door she had painted herself before she realized, and forget to care, how discourteous she was being. Tyffani answered without looking at her sister or, formally inviting her inside, not that she needed to, Teagan stormed across the threshold quite well.

"Where is he," she glowered.

"He just left," Tyffani responded quietly from behind Teagan as she followed her into the kitchen.

"You let him leave," Teagan slammed her fist on the countertop cracking the granite.

"What should I have done? He couldn't stay here; his children think he's dead."

"He will be soon enough you mark my words and if you weren't my own blood I'd send you with him," Teagan spat.

"That will be enough, Teagan Inez Patrick McCarthy."

"Who is going to stop me, you? You couldn't even stop your own husband leaving or, is accomplice a more appropriate term," she narrowed her gaze at her older sister.

"You can either join me upstairs for a mature, adult conversation or, you can leave,"

Tyffani struggled to keep her voice even and inclined her head at the back door when she offered Teagan her choices.

"Upstairs it is then," Teagan responded through gritted teeth.

Tyffani led them to the bedroom she now had all to herself and offered Teagan a seat on the bench at the end of her bed that was made for such things, the younger Princess declined.

"Get on with it then," she tapped her right foot on the hard wood floor.

"Not until you breathe and cool off a bit."

"This is as cool as I'll get so, spill it."

"Listen as my sister please and not as a Detective."

"I'll listen."

"Please hear me Teagan," Tyffani plead.

"I will set aside Detective McCarthy, if you set aside Doctor Davies," Teagan offered.

"Very well, you're not going to like what you're about to hear," Tyffani began telling her everything she herself had only just learned.

Twenty minutes later, having finally taken the seat that was offered her, Teagan absorbed her sister's story with a closed mouth and crossed arms; she was not entirely convinced but, decided to wait until Tyffani had finished before beginning her interrogation.

"So, you were practicing necromancy?"

"No not really. Well kind of but, not the dark stuff. At least not intentionally," she explained, still somewhat confused about it herself.

"There's no such thing as *light* necromancy," Teagan raised a brow.

"Tea, please."

"You did try to bring him back though?"

"Yes but, only that, I wasn't trying to take his soul," Tyffani paced in front of Teagan.

"You do realize that when you did that, you imparted in him a bit of yourself," Teagan condescended.

"I do now, yes."

"That is probably the only thing that saved you."

"I know."

"Why did you try to save him in the first place?"

"I had admired him for a long time. I thought him handsome, good humored, hard working. I thought if I could bring him back, why shouldn't I?"

"Because you had no idea what you were doing," judgement dripping from each word.

"I get that now," Tyffani paused her pacing just in front of her sister, "I'm sorry Teagan."

"Sorry? *You're sorry*," Teagan fumed.

"Yes," she said sheepishly and sat down cross legged in front of Teagan.

"You used magic you didn't understand to bring back a man you didn't know because you had a crush on him and now my husband's life hangs in the balance," Teagan admonished her sister, loudly.

"I know that. Don't you think I know that?"

"I don't doubt that you know it but, I'm not sure you understand it."

"What's that supposed to mean?"

"It means you're acting like you borrowed my favorite pair of jeans without asking and accidentally stained them, you can't undo what's been done."

"Everything is black and white with you. You have no room for grey," Tyffani got up and turned to exit the room.

"It is black and white Tyffani, you fucked up and because you fucked up now everything is fucked up," she got up and stormed passed her sister, "own it."

"That's all I can do," Tyffani yelled back at her, their faces now only inches from each other.

"Well, finally you take responsibility for something. You've been carrying that cross around on your back for the past four months expecting pity from everyone who looks sideways at you, I'm glad you're done being a martyr."

"That's right I've been a martyr. I've wanted sympathy. I have five broken hearted children to look after, a little sympathy shouldn't have been so hard to come by but, somehow you soaked all of that up didn't you *PRINCESS*," she spat at Teagan.

"Princess is right," Teagan grinned cruelly, "don't forget to call me Queen when I get there as well."

"Just because our father chose you as his successor doesn't give you cause to throw it in my face."

"You brought that up not me and perhaps he chose me

because of how pragmatic I am, reason free from passion and all that."

"You seem to be full of both today little sister."

"You have no idea how much restraint I have practiced since stepping foot in your house eldest child."

"Do tell," Tyffani challenged, arms across her chest.

"Excuse me," followed by a knock at the door indicated children had finally made it home, the interruption allowing their tempers to cool.

"Come in," Tyffani called over her shoulder.

"Hey," her oldest son Bryce, the spitting image of his grandmother, said pushing open the door, "I'm not sure what you guys are arguing about, and I honestly don't care but, keep it down would you? We're trying to handle our homework."

"Start the oven please? 425," Tyffani responded flatly. Bryce slammed the door and huffed downstairs, hopefully to start the oven for pizza, Teagan was starving.

"What am I going to do Tea?"

"You? You? What are you going to do? What am I going to do? My son may not ever know his father because of you and you're asking me what you're going to do with practically grown sprites?" Teagan bit her bottom lip and rolled her eyes, irritation written all over her face.

"You know what Teagan? You are so bloody selfish sometimes. I did not do this on purpose. Weren't you listening? I didn't ask for this."

"If you say that you had no idea who Blair really was I believe you, you know I could check if I really wanted to but, that does not excuse the fact that you play a part in this, indirectly or not," Teagan raised a scarlet brow.

"If it makes you feel better check whatever you want," Tyffani offered, tears springing to the corners of her bright blue eyes.

"No need. I wouldn't break that trust," Teagan said quietly, temper finally dissipated.

"Wouldn't you? You have been throwing that weight around a lot lately."

"It's good to remind people now and then what I am capable of doing. Especially if I think those people are in league with The Queen to end my family."

"Even if those you threaten are your family?"

"Yes, even if. Who better to use against a person than their own family? That's exactly the kind of weapon Blair was, my own family used against me."

"I really am gutted over this Teagan."

"I know."

"I hate fighting with you."

"I know me too."

"You get so mean."

"Sometimes the truth is ugly."

"Yes but, you don't have to be."

"I don't know how else to be when nothing makes sense anymore. I have people coming back from the dead left and right today, it's exhausting."

"I'm sorry, for that and for what I did but I was not helping him in any way. I truly did not know who he really was until an hour ago."

"I am sorry for yelling. I was very angry, I actually thought about lighting you on fire."

"You did not!"

"I did."

"I suppose your temper matched with hormones is not a great combination."

"You suppose correctly."

"I love you," Tyffani uncrossed her arms and hugged her very pregnant younger sister.

"Love you too," Teagan mumbled into Tyffani's hair.

"What will you do," Tyffani pulled away, tucking a strand of Teagan's unruly hair back behind her pointed ear.

"Kill the son of a bitch," Teagan said seriously.

"Make it quick."

"I can't promise that."

Tyffani looked down to allow her tears to spill discreetly down her cheeks, looking back up at Teagan she sniffled and looped her arm through her sisters.

"Shall we start pizzas then?"

"Bel's Beard, I thought you'd never ask, I'm starving!"

After two individual sized pizzas and two large bowls of salad with extra garlic vinaigrette, Teagan was finally sated. Sydni, her eldest niece, had volunteered to help her wash dishes while her mother and siblings cleared up the rest of the kitchen. Teagan had always kept a close relationship with all her nieces and nephews but, she and Sydni interacted more like siblings most of the time. She reminded Teagan of her grandmother Inez in personality but, looked like her grandfather William; she was Teagan's height with large dark green eyes, long dark brown hair and her time spent cheering for her school's football team kept her fit and tan. Teagan had spent long summers with her grandmother Patrick as a sprite before she passed away. She missed her often but, never more fiercely than in the summer and the weeks surrounding her birthday and when she spent too much time away from her niece. It had been months since she had spent any time with the Davies, it was too difficult for Teagan but, kids did not understand her distance because they did not know the truth.

Her usually brightly dispositioned niece sulked in with the rest of the dirty dishes just as Teagan had finished filling the sink with hot soapy water, Sydni set them gently down on the counter without making eye contact.

"Hey," Teagan began, "how is your summer going?"

"Fine I guess," Sydni shrugged at her, taking the first of many dishes she would dry.

"You guess?"

"Yeah," she sighed, "I mean my friends don't really want to hang out very much anymore you know?"

"Why not?"

"Because of dad," she said staring down at her dish towel.

"Because they are silly selfish sprites," Teagan asserted.

"I guess," Sydni shrugged.

"What do they know about what happened?"

"Only what I know, which isn't much and doesn't really add up."

"What do you mean?"

"Why was he at the hospital when it was attacked?"

"What do you suspect he was doing there that your mother left out?"

"Nothing I guess."

"You seem to be doing an awful lot of guessing these days."

"Yeah."

"Are you going to be okay?"

"I hope so," Sydni looked over at her for the first time all evening, smiling sadly as tears welled up in her eyes.

"Oh Syd," Teagan stopped scrubbing, dried her hands and scooped her niece to her in a tight hug.

"I just miss him and I can't get a straight answer from mom and we keep hearing all this stuff from everyone," she shook her head and sniffled, tears spilling onto Teagan's shoulder.

"What kind of stuff," still embracing her; Teagan rubbed her back and rocked them both side to side.

"Bad stuff," Sydni pulled away from her aunt.

"Like what," Teagan insisted, wiping tears from Sydni's cheeks.

"What did you mean when you said mom fucked up and now everything is fucked up?"

"First of all, watch your language Sydni Reigh," She chastised her niece.

"You said it! You cuss all the time," she argued.

"Yes but I am 121, you are sixteen, there's a difference," she admonished, hands now on her hips.

"Whatever, I thought you would tell me at least," she rolled her eyes and huffed over to put a stack of dry plates away.

"Grab bowls for Sorbet would you please," Teagan requested.

"Yes ma'am," Sydni sighed heavily.

"Get rid of the attitude while you're over there too."

"Okay," she responded flatly, setting the requested bowls lightly on the counter.

"I'll grab the rest, let everyone know to get in here while the gettin's good," she said as Sydni walked into the family room.

"Okay."

"Sprites," Teagan rolled her eyes at the freezer door. Her family was passing out spoons by the time she had their dessert and scoops situated, their sullen little faces eager for something sweet. She took a deep breath to steady her resolve before giving them answers they desperately wanted and that no one else would give them.

In all her years as an officer, Teagan had grown accustomed to watching hearts break in front of her when she delivered bad news, she never imagined it would be the hearts of her own family she would break and set into telling them a truth their mother could not.

"Your father was a good father and a good husband," She looked sideways at her sister, tears silently streaming down Tyffani's face, "but, he was not who we thought he was..."

The Davies children received the information better than most adults she had dealt with though, there was not a dry eye in the house by the time Teagan had finished. No one had really touched their dessert, their bowls were more melted sorbet and less empty than Teagan would have liked. Sydni walked over to her where she stood at the island and hugged her hard.

"Can we go see Uncle Rylan now please," she asked gently.

"Yes, I think he would like that very much," Teagan smiled down at her, puffy eyes leaking salt water from their crinkled corners.

Birthday

Her family had stayed until the sun went down and only left after much badgering about school nights and unfinished homework from their matriarch. Teagan was dreading being left alone with her father so naturally she took as long to clean up the kitchen as she possibly could. Setting the last of her oversized teacups in its cabinet, she dried her hands and steadied her temper for the conversation she was about to have. Her father was zipping his guitar into its case when she entered her bedroom. He refused to look at her when she sat on the edge of her bed adjacent the chair he was replacing the throw pillow of; Rylan hated that pillow and all throw pillows for that matter but, men cannot always be counted on for good taste. She silently chuckled to herself at her father taking such care to be gentle with something Rylan regularly started pillow fights with.

"I'm sorry I was so dismissive earlier athair."

"You are going through a lot, Rua. It's not right but, I understand what stress can do."

"Yes but, I was rude because I was angry and that is not acceptable."

"It isn't but, you know that, and that's what is important."

"You're just going to give me the standard 'you learned your lesson' dad speech and go?"

"Yes."

"Father, why won't you look at me?"

"I'm sorry," he said, turning away from his packing to face her, "I am not going to stay tonight."

"What? Why? I thought we could talk about whatever was so pressing earlier."

"You were right, it can wait," he said sheepishly.

"I was just being stubborn," she looked down at her hands.

"Yes, well that cannot be helped," he lifted her face with a finger and kissed her forehead, "I know who your mother is."

"Give that woman my love then," she rose to hug him and walk him out.

"I'll do that sure but, there's no need to walk me out daughter. Get comfortable, relax. I trust that you are well guarded, you should too."

"I do. I know you wouldn't leave if you thought otherwise."

"Indeed," he nodded and turned on his heel to leave.

"I love you," she called after him.

"I love you more," he said over his shoulder, "good night."

"Night."

As soon as she heard her front door close, she did just that. Her most comfortable pajamas didn't fit quite like they use to but, she didn't care. Tonight was the first night in months that she had her house all to herself and her little family, Rylan's steady breathing and Airioch's soft snoring, after she had come in from hunting, were the perfect accompaniment to her reading in bed.

She had put the kettle on as soon as her Dragoon had

landed on the back stoop and heated up some of the brownies her sister had brought over the day before. Body transformation aside, she had recently decided that she rather enjoyed being pregnant and would be willing to endure swollen feet and restless nights again whenever Rylan was ready. It was hard to think of him as being in any state aside from sleeping, at least he should be well rested when Rette arrived, Rette who now kicked her for two-minute intervals no less than four times a day. He must have felt her thinking about him because he began such a fit just then, causing her book to bounce on her belly where she had balanced it. Her sudden outburst of laughter woke the snoozing Airioch who only rolled over onto her stomach and glared at Teagan through one sleep gummed eye before her snoring resumed. Completely content for the first time in ages, Teagan drifted to sleep amongst her family with one of her oft read books open on the bed on the last page she had turned; 'Promise me you'll never forget me because if I thought you would, I'd never leave.'

The eerie voice did not wake her immediately when she heard it, Teagan thought she was dreaming, dreaming of a case she had worked years ago where she was chasing a suspect through an alley way behind a hotel. The air was heavy, humid and hot, too sticky for the middle of August when the monsoons had already come and gone.

This is what alerted her that she was no longer dreaming, the voice she was hearing was not a cornered drug addict. She rose slowly from the bed careful not to disturb her husband or, their Dragoon, she quietly opened the wardrobe and withdrew a change of clothes.

If she had to defend her home and her beloved, a camisole

and shorts would not do, she couldn't hide anything in what little she had on, let alone the cache of weapons she usually strapped herself with. She entered the bathroom, shut the door noiselessly and flipped the light on only after the door was secure. She pulled her vest on over her camisole, taking care not to strap it too tightly across her midsection. She pulled a black hoodie over her vest, her black leggings no longer covered her belly as they once did so she was glad she kept her shorts on and that the hoodie was oversized. Turning off the light she grabbed her boots and her katana resting in its holster from the top of the wardrobe. She took one last look at Rylan, breathed deeply, sent him thoughts of love and placed a protection rune over the door after she closed and locked it, stopping at the hall closet to retrieve a few more weapons from her secret stash, she strapped her preferred weapon across her back, pulled her boots on and exited the back of the house. She reached out mentally to check on the officers stationed at random posts throughout the property and felt nothing. She pushed harder and again felt nothing but, this time she heard nothing either. Dread filled her from wing-tip to toe and settled somewhere in her gut, swallowing hard she put up her guards and opened her mind.

She was halfway around the east perimeter when she heard the voice again, louder and more menacing this time.

'Teagan,' it was male, 'come out, come out wherever you are.'

The hairs on the back of her neck were behaving as though she'd stuck her finger in a light socket.

'Teagan,' louder still but, not closer, 'come out and play, won't you?'

The laughter was ominous and more unsettling than the vaguely familiar voice had been. She could not feel who it was, could not hear them or, see their intent.

'Wakey, wakey Princess,' the voice hissed again.

She pushed harder and felt herself being actively blocked. She was stricken suddenly with a terrible realization, Kaius.

She heard an ear-splitting crack from the direction of the house, the protection rune on the back door had been broken and the door along with it no doubt. She turned on her heel and was instantly knocked back. Her head whipped sideways, and she tasted the blood trickling from her busted nose. She heard another loud crack and knew that her bedroom door had been breached, Kaius grabbed her by the hair and dragged her through the gravel to her front yard. She pulled the small dagger she had strapped to her leg from its sheath and stabbed him just above the left knee, she knew that was his weak leg and hoped the poison on the knife worked as quickly as it was meant to. He buckled and let go of her just before they reached the stone pathway that lead to her front door; not that it mattered at this point but, her brother Seth would be glad to know it was still intact. She rolled sideways and flew above her former brother-in-law's head, hanging there like the blade of a guillotine waiting to drop. Kaius glared up at her, locked eyes and refused to look away, he appeared more in his element now than Teagan had ever seen him.

She was glad he was so comfortable, relaxed is how one should go to their death. As she stared into the eyes of her would-be assassin, another image burst across her mind. Splitting her focus, she landed and continued circling her opponent, in her mind's eye she was staring down at her comatose husband in their bed. Rylan's eyes opened abruptly when the sheets were ripped back off of his body, panic truly set in and Teagan knew she had to make quick work of her diversion. Noting the fear on Teagan's face, a menacing grin split across Kaius', Rylan inhaled sharply, the pain of the action doing nothing to assuage Teagan's fear. A woman was standing over him, long dark hair parted down the middle spilled over her shoulders when she bent close to his face. Taking advantage of Teagan's distracted state, Kaius swung his broadsword at her right shoulder, his rapidly deteriorating left leg nearly causing him to miss, she deflected with her Katana reflexively. Small, black eyes bore into Teagan's consciousness, flying upward to dodge another well aimed blow; she took a moment to study the face staring into her husbands. She felt Airioch blaze out of their home and dart straight for Kaius.

'No Airioch! Go back to Rylan.'

'I'm sorry Princess but, I cannot. My duty is to you and your child.'

'No please, I cannot be in two places at once! I can protect myself and Rette but, Rylan needs help!

The terribly beautiful face in her mind's eye opened its duplicitous maw and, if Teagan got her way, spoke the last words she would ever speak.

'A Feandragoon,' she cooed, 'isn't that precious.'

'Tylane.'

'That's Queen Tylane to you Princess,' her butterscotch rich voice oozed condescension.

'Queen? I thought it was Empress? Taken a pay cut have we? Your fight is with me, leave him alone.'

'I would come out and play but, it seems you are quite busy,' she laughed.

'Lucky for you I am an excellent multitasker. Come now, don't be shy.'

'Shy is something I have never been accused of being. You know, one of my Knights had a Feandragoon, didn't help much in saving his soul though.'

Teagan landed hard just behind Kaius, barely avoiding him taking off her foot before she did. He batted Airioch away with a heavy, chainmail gloved hand, the force knocked her to the ground just outside of Teagan's line of sight.

'I told you Dragoons weren't much use, typical youth, thinking they know it all.'

'Typical cowardice, sending your minion to do a job you haven't the stomach for,' Teagan baited her, ignoring the Orion jab.

'Kaius has much simpler tastes than I do. Besides I prefer dessert and your husband smells positively divine,' she inhaled Rylan's musk deeply, eyes closing in anticipation.

'You will leave him be or, I'll kill you, I'll kill your puppet and your entire court before setting your mound on fire,' Teagan warned.

'I don't think you will. I think you will watch me kill the father of your unborn child before Kaius bleeds you in your own back-yard,' Tylane said, stroking Rylan's hair.

Another heavy blow glanced off her Katana as she stood at her full height to meet Kaius' blade with her own. She flew up over him and sliced down at his head, he met it with some effort. She was glad the poison was taking effect, and he was wearing out, broadswords are heavy and cumbersome as was the man who happened to be wielding this particular sword.

'*Leave him alone Tylane,*' Teagan warned again, she tried with all the energy she could spare to freeze Tylane like the medusa she was.

'*Tsk Tsk Princess,*' she clucked, '*your mind tricks will not work on me.*'

'*Keep telling yourself that,*' Teagan attempted again, making herself dizzy from the effort.

'*Should you survive this night, which I very highly doubt, ask your beloved father why you and yours must die,*' she drew a long thin knife from a scabbard at her waist, pulling Rylan's white blonde hair back so hard he winced even in his comatose state and his neck twisted at an odd angle.

'*Say goodbye Teagan, 'goodbye Teagan',* she mimicked Rylan's voice, laughing wickedly as she cut his throat.

Flight

There are four possible responses in the brain when confronted with attack; Fight, flight posture and submit. When he and Teagan were attacked while leaving the hospital, he had chosen to fight, after they arrived safely home he ventured a posture. He would never submit, not to this nasty worm attempting to bore holes in his synapses. Flight it must be then.

He came to just in time to see her one last time and wished he hadn't. The pain, her pain, was overwhelming; it washed over him like monsoon rain floods a thirsty Tucson wash mid-July. It dwarfed the physical pain he felt momentarily before his death. All the life he'd had. All the great experiences, all the bad ones, all the pain and loss that fill more than a hundred years. He had lived. One final breath, deep, searing pain as his throat was sliced open brutally and then, lights out. Teagan, Teagan, Teagan and her anguish, her rage. He thought about the poor sod who would feel her fury and could only chuckle. He felt nothing now, he felt *like* nothing, light as air. He was floating, which was not flying but was very lovely. He loved flying though he didn't have wings. Teagan did and she flew them anywhere they wished. Always. She made him fly.

When he felt so small he couldn't fill a thimble, she found room to sit with him there.

When he forgot who he was, Teagan remembered for them both and lead him out of his darkness. She always thought herself thunder but, to him she was a rainbow. He felt something viscous at his fingertips, then his toes and his hair. It seemed too thick to be water but, felt like water...

"It is water," Rylan opened his eyes to discover an interesting being, who likely didn't know how loud she was.

"I am not actually loud, all of your tissue is new so, everything is extra sensitive," she informed him, pastel violet eyes smiling.

Rylan recognized her as Banshee, the horrific exposed tooth and bone grin was marker enough. He made to sit up and she rushed to guide him so he didn't go too fast too soon; everything was sore and stiff so movement came slowly to his limbs even without guide of a Banshee.

"Thank you," he said, his own voice sounded too loud in his head.

"I warned you," she chuckled, a tinkling bell of a sound.

He only smiled in answer.

"We are, of course, very pleased that you've made it," she began, "it is quite unusual, and I am sorry to hustle you along but, you do have a meeting soon."

"Who could the new guy possibly need to meet," he joked.

"Me," a gravel deep voice greeted him, just above a whisper.

A well-built, auburn bearded man slowly made his way toward him.

"We have a great deal to discuss and very little time to do so, Rylan McCarthy," the man with whom he would be meeting handed him a pile of clean linen clothing, "it can wait only as long as it takes you to dress. Be a shame to meet your son in such a state now, wouldn't it."

Rylan's face crumpled with the full range of emotion that overcame him as tears streamed down his cheeks.

"Come now sir, I'll help," the Banshee held him up while the auburn bearded man helped him into his clothes.

"Who," Rylan hiccupped "who are you?"

"My name is Rory er, Aurora," the grey-haired banshee said.

"Aurora, no offense but, I was asking him."

The green velvet attired man scratched the chin beneath his beard, grinned broadly and said, "I am Bel."

Rylan lost what little control he had over his knees and fell hard back onto the bed he had just been stood up from.

Teagan fell to her knees as another potentially fatal blow sheared where her neck had been a mere moment before, her heart was in her throat, blood boiling through her veins as her husband's flowed down his neck soaking his shirt and their bed sheets. Everything went dark, all she could see was Kaius' triumphant expression at what he thought would be a final stroke hacked into Teagan's left shoulder when she darted right and lost grip on her Katana. He raised his weapon to attempt again at splitting her skull in two but, faltered momentarily when he caught the expression on the face of his prey, Teagan glared up at her assailant and had never seen such fear in her life.

His minor misstep was all she needed; left shoulder painfully dislocated, she forced her left hand to grab Kaius' breastplate and pull herself up while bringing him down, an animalistic cry ripping from her lungs as she did so. She took the Sai she kept at her side and drove it into his gut with everything she had left, hearing his spine crack as his face came level with hers; hilt deep, she twisted the blade before pulling it back out of his wretched body, blood and guts sprang from his mangled core as he fell lifeless to the rough gravel he previously stood on. She dropped her Sai and fell sideways onto her right hip, looking down at her hands, she was reminded of the poppy fields she and her family had visited in Geneva during her thirtieth birthday celebration. She started laughing and crying hysterically, her son kicked her harder than he ever had, his little heel landing right on her bladder and that began to leak as well.

Airioch, having regained consciousness after the stunning blow she'd received, had burned a ring of white fire around she and Teagan for protection and was sitting just in front of her Faerie scanning the dark for any more unwelcome guests, she glowed as white with anger as the fire she had just set and smoke roiled from her nostrils with each growled exhale. As life and death were making themselves overwhelmingly apparent Galen and the cavalry arrived, just in time to witness their Princess falling apart.

Epilogue

My Dearest Teagan,

It has been months since last we spoke. I do not know if we ever will speak again but, I wanted to write you now because tomorrow I leave for France and for my part in the war. I know it is not fair of me to tell you so but I have missed you. I have missed your humour. I have missed your fierceness. I have missed your smell. Soldiers smell like mud and sweat; you smell like rain falling on wild anise. I have missed your crazy scarlet hair; it's the loveliest red in all the world. I miss you. I am so sorry my love that I must inflict that upon you as I'm sure you've moved on by now and no longer waste a passing thought on me. If I am lucky enough to make it back in one piece, I will come home to you; provided you do still think on me and will still have me. I hope you will still have me. I hope you can find a way to forgive my absence and to love me as you once did; 1914 was a very good year. I hope someday you will know beyond the shadow of a doubt that the only reason I broke communication was because of who I have become; I have had to do unspeakable things since last I saw you and I fear I am no

217

longer the man I once was. I hope that your father will still allow me to marry you; he has already agreed to that once but I will ask every day for the rest of our lives if I must. I will never stop loving you, my Teagan. Me Anam. Me Croi.

Yours Always,

RM

With shaky hands Matthew McCarthy folded the letter he found in his little brothers' uniform jacket, the jacket he would be buried in, and placed it back in the pocket where he had found it. Nearly one hundred years later and it still smelled faintly of Rylan; cherry tobacco, cardamom and vetiver. He let his tears fall freely down his cheeks as he finished gathering burial clothes and cursed his brother for leaving him too soon. They always joked about who would go first; Rylan assumed it would be him due to his recklessness but stood firm that Meagan would send Matt to an early grave if he kept up his foolishness.

"What's that," his pregnant wife asked, looking up from the bed where she sat folding clothes.

"Oh, it's nothing," he lied, closing the heavy closet door.

"Mmhmm, I know that tone Matthew Bryan," she scoffed and with some effort, stood up to meet him when he turned from his brother's wardrobe to face her.

"It was a letter to Teagan," he looked down at his hands, "it was unopened."

"She should read it then," Meagan insisted.

"Should she? She is barely with us as it is, this might break her," he exhaled heavily.

"It might bring her back," Meagan suggested, taking her husband's hands in her own.

"You know her better."

"I'm not sure even Teagan knows this version of herself," she guided them back to sit on the edge of their siblings' bed.

"Don't be so quick to judge little one," Matt quietly defended his sister-in-law.

"I'm judging a little bit. It's not just herself she has to worry about anymore," Meagan went on the offense, "besides, Rylan would not recognize this Teagan either."

"No but, he wouldn't blame or judge her either," Matt sighed at his wife's harshness.

"No one blames her Matthew."

"There's no need to, she blames herself enough as it is."

"Give her the letter."

"I'll think about it," Matt kissed the back of Meagan's hand and carried his guilt from the room along with his brother's funeral garb, leaving his wife to fold their nephew's laundry.

An excerpt from Moxie, book two of The Southwest Faerie Chronicles:

Ruined

Teagan rolled over onto her back and pushed the hair out of her face. She had had the same dream every night for almost four years. She would always go back to the day her family had brought her back from the dead. Her Rylan and her Rette. Her soul and her heart. She would always be grateful they had chosen her. She would always lament the loss of her soul. She stretched before getting out of bed to relieve herself and then went to the kitchen to make some tea. She was begrudgingly aware that she would have a visitor soon and not the sort she appreciated in the middle of her sleep.

She knew before answering the door who would be on the other side of it. Standing before her was her mother, Rose Hagan Patrick. The image of beautiful Faerie Queen in the flesh, she was wearing a dark red travelling cloak Teagan had given her for Winter Solstice many years before and a concerned expression on her flawless face.

"The kettle is on. Close the door behind you please," Teagan said as she padded softly back into the kitchen. Her mother knocked the ice from her boots, hung her cloak and closed the back door in silence as her daughter set out teacups, she headed over to the drawer to procure tea cozies.

"You know why I am here," her mother said to her back.

"Yes," Teagan replied stiffly, "do you still take honey in your English Breakfast?"

"I do," Rose answered just as the kettle whistled that it was ready.

Perched straight backed with ankles crossed in a kitchen chair her dearly departed Son in Law had made himself, red leather gloved hands folded on her lap, Rose was grateful for the fire that burned in the living room hearth whose warmth permeated every inch of the house. She knew it was something Teagan had carried with her from sprite hood, during the winter months Teagan slept in front of the fire more often than her own bed and usually woke up a smiling, sweaty, sooty mess.

"It does feel a bit like my youth, doesn't it? Perhaps if I'd made hot chocolate instead," the Princess mused, "No matter. Please begin mother. I know this is not a short story and I would like to go back to sleep as soon as possible."

The Queen knew Teagan was trying to be hurtful. She was behaving like an injured animal lashing out at her perceived abusers as a result of the trauma she had endured. It was something she'd always done, been mean on purpose when she was in emotional pain. Articulating what she was feeling had never come easily nor had it ever been comfortable for Tea, it was something she had always had to work on and now was not the time to correct her child. Now was the time for love and for explanations. She reminded herself how much she loved her stubborn, heartbroken child and began what she was there to tell.

"Fiona foresaw that The Seventh child of The Third Patrick King would be the undoing of the UnSeelie Empress, you know her as Tylane DeKawley. You've seen her, she killed your husband. She was also your father's first wife. She believed that if the child prophesied was born to her, she could make the child love her or, she would kill it. After Fiona revealed to her, her fate, Tylane killed The Oracle and began scheming ways to find herself in your father's good graces. They married eventually, much to your grandfather William's chagrin, and were pregnant very shortly after. Tylane got pregnant several times and miscarried each child, her womb as rotten as her soul no doubt. The seventh and final time, she told your father of Fiona's vision while their child bled from her body. Disgusted with Tylane and horrified that he had been so blind, he helped her heal, annulled their marriage and then disowned her. Shunned and humiliated, she ran home to her Mother in The Winterlands. Soon after, The UnSeelie court declared war on The Salann. It was a brutal affair and was drawn out far longer

than anyone anticipated. Queen Khora had the same hate in her heart that her daughter does, and she had no end of Knights willing to do her bidding. Changelings more like. I often wonder how many humans unknowingly sacrificed their children to that war in exchange for hollow shells that had their loved ones faces. Though they prevailed, your aunt and grandfather were slain and the disgraced Empress was nowhere to be found, leaving your father to rebuild a ravaged kingdom alone.

That's when we met. Though my father was Sulach, as you know Sulach and Salann have always gotten along well, being lesser Fae makes it easy to ignore the nonsense that being part of the formal courts entails and allowed them to enjoy being Faeries. Oh, they still got up to plenty of mischief mind you but, certainly nothing malicious as some Fae are wont to do.

When Kingship was thrust upon him, your father sought council with your grandfather Hagan. They became fast friends and would strategize long into the night nearly every night it seemed," she paused at this to catch her breath and for a sip of tea. Smiling at the memory of sleepy Timothy Patrick exiting her father's study in the wee hours of a morning 200 years before, Queen Patrick began speaking again with renewed fervor.

"I would make him breakfast in the morning before he left for home and we would speak as young Folk often do, of bright futures and happy memories. He was depressed about having lost his family and had a difficult time speaking about it. Something I've always appreciated about your father is his ability to treat people as they are, he doesn't take out his bitterness or disappointment on anyone. He is easy to love, your father, and our courtship was short. For years after the war there were rumors of Tylane being everywhere. They grew more frequent when we married and with each subsequent child.

In the summer of 1878, I gave birth to our sixth child. He was beautiful, my Liam, he looked just like your father. Only three months he lived and then passed suddenly in his sleep. You have never seen a baby coffin and I pray you never have to. They're so small. It's hard to imagine anything so tiny needing to be buried. Like whatever lay inside it hasn't been around long enough to have earned death. He looked like a little porcelain doll, as though he were waiting in a shop and the right amount of love would make him a real boy again," she stopped for a moment to wipe away tears and continued with eyes down cast, "When we got pregnant with you, we were so happy my darling. We knew you would survive, knew your fate. So did Tylane."

"The lamb for slaughter," Teagan seethed, "I am glad, mother, that you have your family and mine was the cost of your happiness. Father may not take his bitterness out on others but, I know exactly where mine should be directed. Please leave, I will see you and father again when I am ready." Teagan cleared their half full teacups and put them in the sink as her mother stood to protest.

"What about Everette," Rose pleaded.

"What *about* Everette mother?"

"He deserves to know who his grandparents are."

"No," Teagan began, anger flushing her pale cheeks, "he deserved to know who his father was but, you took that from him didn't you?"

"There was nothing could be done."

"You could've told me! You could've told *me* so I wouldn't bring anyone else into my life until I did what I was born to do. You could have been honest about why I trained harder with Trinity than even my brothers did. You have always known of my gift and both you and father purposely kept *this* from me. 'Secrets rot away the foundation of trust', isn't that what you always told us?"

"You're right, we did," Rose looked down at her hands, drained and defeated "I am sorry for your pain my darling, truly I am but, I would never prevent you from love. You cannot tell me you regret your son, that you regret your many years with your lover, that you would really have made a different decision about Rylan."

"I should have been given the choice," Teagan said barely above a whisper, angry tears streaming down her face.

The Queen took her daughter in her arms and held her tight while she silently cried on her shoulder.

"I love you Teagan Inez," she whispered, stroking Teagan's long scarlet hair.

"He is awake," Teagan pushed away, "go, now."

Jess Torres Photography

Maggie was born and raised in Arizona, loves travel, tacos and hopes you'll tell your dog she says hello. In addition to writing, she co-hosts a mental health/comedy podcast, Which Dog Are You Today, and is probably at the local coffee house or baking a Hollywood Handshake worthy pumpkin roll. This is her debut novel. Instagram: @maggs_the_rad, @wdayt_pod

Milton Keynes UK
Ingram Content Group UK Ltd.
UKHW041148250424
441684UK00004B/50

9 798990 422100